THE RECORD OF MY HEART

GEORGINA GUTHRIE

OMNIFIC PUBLISHING
LOS ANGELES

Omnific Publishing
1901 Avenue of the Stars, 2nd floor
Los Angeles, CA 90067
www.omnificpublishing.com

First Omnific eBook edition, March 2015
First Omnific trade paperback edition, March 2015

The characters and events in this book are fictitious.
Any similarity to real persons, living or dead,
is coincidental and not intended by the author.

Library of Congress Cataloguing-in-Publication Data

Guthrie, Georgina.
   The Record of My Heart / Georgina Guthrie – 1st ed.
   ISBN: 978-1-623422-18-9
   1. Contemporary Romance — Fiction. 2. University — Fiction.
   3. Shakespeare — Fiction. 4. Love Letters — Fiction. I. Title

10 9 8 7 6 5 4 3 2 1

Cover Design by Micha Stone and Amy Brokaw
Interior Book Design by Coreen Montagna

Printed in the United States of America

Michelle I. Tompkins
Inspired by Words, 2010, mixed media collage
Private collection

…thus begins the record of our hearts…
(Rabindranath Tagore, *The Gardener*)

Preface

My beautiful Aubrey,

You are, no doubt, wondering what this book I've thrust into your hands is all about. Let me explain, sweetheart. Do you remember the documents I saved onto your Kindle...the ones you read on the plane to England? When I gave you those files, sharing only a couple of weeks of my private reflections from the beginning of the semester, I may have misled you into believing that I ceased journaling once we had declared our intentions to pursue a relationship. This couldn't be further from the truth.

My dispassionate descriptions of our initial encounters swiftly progressed beyond banal documentation, eventually becoming the secret musings of a man tumbling headfirst in love with you. In short, Aubrey, you are holding a book of love, what the Bard might call "a volume of enticing lines," which traces the stirrings of my heart in the first weeks and months of our relationship with nothing glossed over. I had the pages professionally bound, thinking this might be a nice keepsake for us to look back on in the years to come.

The fact that you are reading the preface to this book means that the evening we've just spent out together has gone favorably for me, and you are now my fiancée. And so, tonight, on the first evening of our engagement, do you dare look more deeply into the heart of the man who wants to spend his life making you the happiest woman in the world? If so, then please read on.

On second thought, come to bed with me, poppet. There will be plenty of time for reading in the morning...
Forever yours,
Daniel

xoxoxo...

Part One

The Joys of Trying to Cover Your Ass
When You're Falling in Love with a Student
and Don't Know It

STUDENT: AUBREY PRICE

First day of semester: Monday, February 2

(Here I remind you to brace yourself, poppet. I considered omitting this set of entries, but that would be cowardly…it's probably just as cowardly to editorialize all of the asinine comments I made early in the semester, but I simply can't let them stand without some sort of explanation. Forgive me.)

If my experiences last year taught me nothing else, they certainly underscored the importance of carefully documenting my exchanges with female students, especially those exchanges that make me feel uneasy. I'm remembering a piece of advice my grandfather used to share: *If something unsettles you, there's probably good cause. Those hairs were put on the back of your neck for a reason.*

So here I sit, on the first day of the semester, already feeling unsettled. I met Martin's class today. Aside from arriving late for the lecture (thanks to another argument with my father), the class was fairly unremarkable — just your average fourth-year Shakespeare course. Having said that, there is a student in the class with whom I feel strangely compelled to proceed with caution.

Her name is Aubrey Price, and when she looked at me at the end of the lecture, those telltale hairs on my neck sent me a strong message — something along the lines of "clear and present danger." I had glanced her way briefly, wanting to acknowledge her class participation, but there was a strange glint in her eye as she looked back at me — challenging me? Appraising me? It was a wholly unnerving feeling.

I reviewed the student files Martin gave me. Miss Price has an impressive GPA; in class she appeared bright and outspoken. There's evidence of a history with Martin. I'll have to ask him more about her. I can't put my finger on the reason why, but I feel as if I'll need to keep my wits about me with this one.

(Notice here, sweetheart, how I've completely omitted any mention of how beautiful I thought your eyes were when you gazed across the room at me, your lovely graceful neck and luminous skin so striking, setting you apart from your peers. Of course, there's also the fact that I had to wipe the drool from my mouth when you stood up and I caught a glimpse of your fantastic ass and long legs in those insanely tight jeans. You saw me shuffling those papers around at the front of the room. The hairs at the back of my neck weren't the only things standing at attention. Believe me, if I could've left right away without making a spectacle of myself, I would have.)

TUESDAY, FEBRUARY 3

Crossed paths with the Price girl this morning outside the tutorial room. Turns out she works for my father at Victoria! I must be careful to avoid using this common relationship as a breeding ground for "friendship." Our exchange left me feeling ill at ease, yet again. She was blushing and awkward—tongue-tied, even. Either she's a social misfit (which seems unlikely), or she felt uncomfortable talking to me for some reason. I'm trying not to jump to conclusions. I made a speedy exit so I wouldn't get drawn into a more personal conversation.

Unfortunately, I bumped into her at the coffee shop in Hart House no more than half an hour later and had another exchange with her. While I tried not to push the envelope with familiarity, I'm not sure how successful I was. (Note: room was full of patrons.) Again, she successfully identified a passage—"For some must watch while some must sleep; thus runs the world away" which isn't exactly a quotation that lives on in infamy. (She's no academic slouch, that's for sure. Or she simply has a bizarre photographic memory where *Hamlet* is concerned.)

Then, I saw her again this afternoon at Vic. I was returning from a late lunch with my father, both of us annoyed after yet another argument. The sight of Miss Price approaching from the Lower House residences made me feel even more agitated.

(Agitated? That's one way of putting it. How else could I put into words the overwhelming desire to pull you into my arms and kiss you on the second day of our acquaintance? And damn you for blushing so beautifully over your coffee cup, identifying that Hamlet quotation so easily and biting your lip while doing it! Let's not even get into the fact that you were wearing your black yoga pants that day. Were you trying to kill me?)

I continue to have this vague, unsettled feeling. Why do I keep running into her? It's as if she's spying on me…like she's been assigned to watch me, maybe even to "test" me. Even as I write this, I realize the complete absurdity of the notion, but who knows the lengths a university administration would pursue in order to verify the reputation of a TA with a checkered past?

(I read this now, and I want to die of mortification. How could I have even speculated that you were some sort of a spy? What a knob.)

Another awkward encounter with Miss Price. I kept her after Martin's lecture to request that she not mention our in-class relationship to my father. I don't want to get pulled into some strange three-way entanglement. That's what I told her, anyway. She seemed aggravated—maybe even angry—but I couldn't bring myself to feel remorseful. Her annoyance is a good thing. I was too familiar yesterday, so it didn't hurt to rein things in a bit. Worth noting: the door was wide open.

(You know what was motivating me on this day was the fear that my father would discover I knew you from Martin's class – right on the heels of him suggesting I meet the intelligent, attractive girl who worked in his office. I'm sorry I was nasty to you. Pushing you away that day seemed preferable to giving my father an acute angina attack.)

During today's lecture, I found myself again thinking about Miss Price and the fact that she's not just a student in the class, but also my father's employee. Reflecting on what I told her yesterday about my father, I began to wonder — what if *he* somehow roped her into taking the course to watch me? Or, I thought, perhaps he surveyed the class enrollment in September and found a student in need of employment and hired her so he could have someone to report back to him once second semester rolled around?

After the tutorial, though, I felt confident concluding that Miss Price is a serious scholar. Her observations and inquiry questions were astute, and revealed an interest in the topic beyond that of the casual student of Shakespeare. I feel idiotic (and somewhat egocentric, for that matter) for imagining that someone would take a fourth-year Shakespearean course simply to spy on the class TA.

There was a panicky moment at the end of the seminar as Cara Switzer requested to speak to me alone. Now *there's* a student I don't want to find myself alone with. I asked Miss Price to remain behind, simply as a buffer. I could have asked anyone, but her name came to my lips first. Of course, when I had to explain why I'd asked her to stay behind, I couldn't think of a valid reason and cobbled together some harebrained excuse about lending her books. I was decidedly curt with her. I'd go as far as to say I was rude.

I felt so rattled after the tutorial session that I went straight to Martin's office to chat about a few of the students in the class, bringing Miss Price's name up, among several others. According to Martin, she's been working for my father since September. Martin even wrote her a glowing letter of recommendation when she applied for the job, based on the rapport they developed in prior course studies. He spoke very highly of her, claiming she's "one of those students who walks through your door only a few times in a career," and that I should count myself lucky to be able to work with her.

I'm not feeling very lucky at the moment. I'm feeling remarkably uncomfortable. Not sure what it is about this girl that has me so addled.

(Not sure? Ha! Could it be that I was a mess because your strength and outspokenness in that first tutorial intrigued the hell out of me, but I was forced to distance myself from you? Aubrey, I wanted nothing more than to ask you to stay after Cara had left so that I could close the door, take your hand and say, "Tell me all about yourself – spare no details." Of course, I couldn't do that, which enraged me. So instead, I was rude and obnoxious. I hated myself for the way I treated you that day. Self-preservation, plain and simple. I used you to protect myself from Cara, but you didn't know that at the time. You looked so hurt and I felt like a frigging heel. How I wish I could go back and smack some sense into myself...)

WEDNESDAY, FEBRUARY 11

An uneventful week thus far. No further encounters with Miss Price. She seems intent on ignoring me now. There is a sort of weary defiance in her eyes that doesn't sit quite right, but my coolness seems to have curtailed any excessive familiarity that might have had the potential of developing. My father would be proud.

(How it pained me to see the coldness in your eyes. I hated my father that week.)

FRIDAY, FEBRUARY 13

What a strange afternoon. Miss Price looked terrible during class and barely spoke a word during today's tutorial session. Disappointing. I was looking forward to her views on Petruchio's attitudes and behavior. She actually seemed bored, doodling and sighing as if sitting in that room was some incredibly painful form of torture. What can I do? I can't force her to participate and it's ultimately her mark that will suffer. Will she be as surly and disinterested this evening, I wonder.

> (I couldn't have cared less about your goddamn participation marks. I just wanted to hear you speak. But you looked so world-weary. Worst of all, I was afraid your behavior was my fault for treating you so poorly, but was equally terrified of allowing myself to believe that my actions and words could possibly have any bearing on your mood or attitude. The implications of acknowledging that scared the shit out of me – and made me feel like an egotistical prick...)

Update: Friday, February 13, 10 p.m.

I was forced to attend tonight's performance of *Hamlet* alone with Miss Price because Miss Harper had taken ill. This was a circumstance beyond my control, but we were in public, after all, and the outing was related to curricular assessment. Unfortunately, she became quite sick during the performance, and I was forced to drive her home. I placed her safely in the care of a roommate, Matt. There was no need to enter her building. I wouldn't have allowed her entry into my car were it not for the fact that she would quite clearly have had difficulty getting home without my assistance…

Part Two

Uncovering Your Ass
and Learning to Enjoy It

Oh, hell. What the fuck am I doing??? Denial. I've been in an absolute state of denial, completely and utterly disregarding my interest in Aubrey Price. So cool, so professional, so detached. Ha! How superior I've been, "fearing" *she* might be attracted to *me*, worried that she might be harboring some sort of crush on me — Daniel Grant — the handsome, young TA.

I can't deny the truth any longer. The only thing I've feared or worried about is that she might not give me more than a second glance, because I've given her several glances, and they've virtually ALL been inappropriate. For almost two weeks I've been congratulating myself for remaining distant and for keeping Aubrey at arm's length, but let's face it. I'm completely taken with her.

She's beautiful, but there's so much more to her than that. She's intelligent and funny — no, not simply funny — *witty…clever*. I gather from talking to Martin that she's independent and self-sufficient, and watching her interact with her peers shows that she's warm and well-liked. This combination of qualities goes well beyond my kryptonite…

If I didn't understand my feelings before, the truth hit me like a fucking freight train tonight. I almost jumped for joy when Aubrey told me that Julie Harper had taken ill and wouldn't be joining us at the show. There we were, in that theater, watching a play for co-curricular credit, and I actually felt like we were on a *date*. What a moron I am.

Every time she leaned over to tell me something, I felt her breath on my cheek and wanted to still her face with my hand and find her lips in the darkness. Aubrey has the most delicious looking rosebud lips. Oh yes. I've noticed. Have I ever. (Writing that—just *Aubrey*—all I can think about is how I'd love to brush my lips against her cheek and whisper her beautiful name in her ear…Jesus.)

When she got sick, I was useless. I went into panic mode. What if someone had seen us walking together to my car? What if I'd gotten caught driving her home? On the one hand, I'm glad I had the wherewithal to feel alarmed by the implications of my behavior; on the other hand, I can't believe I allowed Nicola's accusations and my experiences at Oxford to dictate my actions so completely. I was a total boor. My reaction was a defensive mechanism, of course, but Aubrey must think I'm an asshole, and if she doesn't, she's a frigging saint.

Actually, what am I thinking? She's probably not giving me a second thought. This guy…this Matt…he was waiting for her when I dropped her off. He practically lifted her into his arms like some sort of fucking knight in shining armor. He'd literally run back to Jackman Hall from a party to be there for her when she got home. How can I compete with that? I can't even talk to her alone in a room for fear of reprisals. Christ, I'm afraid to even refer to her by her first name!

Acknowledging my frustration that he has what I can't even get *close* to, makes it impossible for me to continue denying my feelings. So here I am, two weeks into the semester and already careening toward disaster, unable to share my predicament with anyone, my computer screen the only safe place to vent.

As I sit here contemplating this mess I've gotten myself into, I can't help thinking maybe I deserved what happened at Oxford. Perhaps I did give Nicola the wrong idea. What if her accusations were exacerbated by some sort of inappropriate behavior on my part?

Bottom line: I am screwed and it's my own damn fault. I've lost my moral compass, and when I close my eyes to try to center myself—as indeed I'm doing right this very minute—all I see are Aubrey's sparkling green eyes looking back at me…

SATURDAY, FEBRUARY 14

Sad sack that I am, I spent Valentine's Day with Penny. Not that I don't love the girl, but really, what a pathetic state of affairs. Things might have been worse, I guess. I could have gone out with Jeremy. I had myself convinced that I was doing Penn a favor by meeting her for dinner to keep her company while Brad's out of town, but let's face it—I was the one in need of distracting this evening.

All I could think about was Aubrey, wondering if she was feeling all right after last night's craziness, and obsessing about whether she might be out somewhere with her "roommate," enjoying Valentine's Day. I felt physically sick at the thought. Would Matt buy chocolates? Flowers? Maybe take her out for dinner and a movie? And then afterward…shit. The thoughts that flood my mind when I imagine them together—there's not enough brain bleach in the world, I fucking kid you not.

So, thank God for Penny. We met at Canoe, and she sat and listened as I shared my pathetic tale—carefully, mind you. I made no mention of Aubrey's name and didn't reveal that she works for my father, only the fact that she's just a student. (*Just* a student! Ha! Listen to me! I've lost my fucking mind, I'm sure of it…)

Penny promised to keep my secret, even from Brad. I don't want to put him in an awkward situation. Of course, that doesn't mean Penny isn't in one hell of a position…

You know, after everything she's put up with over the last year and a half, I'm amazed Penny is still prepared to spend time with me. I'm not sure what I've done to deserve her friendship and loyalty, but maybe she figures there's no point writing me off. Soon she'll be my sister-in-law, and then there's no escaping me.

Penn's advice was predictable. She told me I have to put thoughts of "this girl" out of my mind and remember she could ruin me if I allowed myself to cross a line. She reminded me that I've been given a second chance, and if I screw up, I'll have no one but myself to blame. She also made me feel like a complete prat, pointing out that I've known the girl for all of two weeks and I'm pining for her like a pimply fourteen-year-old! She's right. What the hell is my problem?

I'm truly at a loss to understand what it is about Aubrey that affects me so profoundly. Maybe I'm just starved for female companionship. After being unattached, frozen emotionally for almost a year, perhaps I'm finally starting to thaw. Then in walks Aubrey, who is warm and intelligent, beautiful and sexy, and I'm blindsided.

To top it all off, we do seem to have some sort of strange chemistry—something I haven't felt in a long time. It can't be possible that I was imagining the undercurrent between us last night. But perhaps I'm overreacting, since it's been so long since I've felt connected to anyone. Given the fact that she clearly has a boyfriend, I must be reading into things. Simply put, where this perceived connection between us is concerned, I'm seeing what I want to see.

Chemistry or not, Penny is right. I have to steer well clear of her. I have to put an end to these futile fantasies. Come Monday morning, I will be everything my father has advised: helpful and interested in Aubrey's work, but emotionally detached. This is how it has to be if I hope to protect my position at the university and preserve my sanity.

What I really need is a diversion. I'm tempted to call Sabrina. Desperate times call for desperate measures.

But really, what would be the harm? I need a friend, and she was supportive when I came home from the UK, telling me she'd always be there for me if I needed her. All I know is that I have to *do* something. All this overthinking is killing me. A trip to Ottawa might be fun. We could take in a few museums, hit up some good restaurants…

Yes, I'll call Sabrina—not tonight, though—a Valentine's Day call might be misconstrued. I'll call her tomorrow. I feel better already, just having made a decision.

SUNDAY, FEBRUARY 15

I phoned Sabrina today. I can't decide how I feel about our talk. I have the distinct impression I've leaped from the frying pan smack dab into the middle of the fire. When I mentioned a trip to Ottawa to visit her, I swear I heard her exhale—a long, low sigh—a sigh of victory perhaps, as if she'd been waiting for me to utter those very words since she left for Ottawa at Christmastime. I should have left well enough alone. As she breathed out, I felt my own chest tighten, and the rest of the conversation was a jumble of words competing with the shrieking inside my brain, something to the tune of "WHAT IN THE LIVING FUCK ARE YOU DOING?"

But there I go, overanalyzing again. In fact, allowing myself to believe she's so eager to see me makes me sound like an arrogant git. In what way is securing my attention a victory? I'm a mess, and if she knew better, she'd keep her distance. Either she doesn't know better or she's just as desperate for companionship as I am…

MONDAY, FEBRUARY 16

How many sensations can one woman provoke in the course of an hour? In the case of Aubrey Price, apparently a metric fuckton. She gave me an emotional workout this morning, handing me my ass in the process.

First, there was anger. I arrived at my dad's office to look for him after he didn't show up for our coffee meeting, only to find Aubrey alone in his private office, rooting through his desk. What the hell was she doing in there alone? My father would be horrified at the thought that she was in there without his approval. (Add to that the panic I felt, being alone in that office with her without any witnesses… imagine my first thoughts. I lost all ability to be rational.)

Next came embarrassment. As it turned out, her reason for being in my father's office was not just legitimate, but sanctioned by him. He'd been called away and she was helping him find some documents in his filing cabinet. He confirmed as much when I phoned him. I had needlessly lost my temper and made a buffoon of myself. Great.

Shame followed. She could have been a bitch and thrown my words and accusations back at me, but she immediately brushed my behavior aside, claiming I'd made an honest mistake.

Finally, I settled into a state of gratitude. Not only did she forgive my asinine behavior, she listened to me as I waxed on about my brothers and my friendship with Penny. I completely forgot myself with her. I could have sat and chatted with her for hours. She was so frigging receptive to my jabbering, I swear I was on the verge of telling her all about what happened at Oxford. Luckily, I caught myself in time and got the hell out of there.

(But not before allowing myself to believe she'd enjoyed our chat as much as I had. So, I suppose you can add *delusional* to the emotional catalog of my day.)

And now, I'm left thinking that all the qualities I'm observing in Aubrey (some borne of attraction — I won't attempt to deny it — but others based on her actions and words), would make her an amazing friend and confidante. I can imagine her listening quietly and nodding sympathetically as I pour out my soul to her. The thought of doing that, however fantastical and ill-advised the notion is, makes me feel strangely content.

If I could speak to her now, perhaps wax poetic, I'd share a sonnet with her — one which I'm identifying with in a completely different way tonight. It makes more sense to me now than it ever has before…

Sonnet 29

"When, in disgrace with fortune and men's eyes,
I all alone beweep my outcast state
And trouble deaf heaven with my bootless cries
And look upon myself and curse my fate,
Wishing me like to one more rich in hope,
Featured like him, like him with friends possess'd,
Desiring this man's art and that man's scope,
With what I most enjoy contented least;
Yet in these thoughts myself almost despising,
Haply I think on thee, and then my state,
Like to the lark at break of day arising
From sullen earth, sings hymns at heaven's gate;
For thy sweet love remember'd such wealth brings
That then I scorn to change my state with kings."

~ W. Shakespeare

"I think on thee…and then my state…sings hymns at heaven's gate…" God, how I wish I could feel this way when I think of Sabrina (or anyone but Aubrey, for that matter). That would be so very convenient.

Holy shit, what a week! I've been going non-stop. I guess pre-Reading Week panic set in because I found myself meeting with students in every spare minute, with conferences not just filling my office hours, but going well beyond my required time. Some of these students need a hell of a lot of guidance. It feels good to know I can genuinely help. Having the opportunity to meet with Aubrey and spend some one-on-one time with her would have been the icing on the cake, but I sense she's not remotely in need of my assistance. Case in point, today's tutorial…

I asked everyone to find their favorite quotation from *Macbeth* and then justify their choice. Everyone opened their books to find a good line—everyone except Aubrey, that is. She simply picked up her pen and wrote down a quotation without even cracking the play open. For an undergrad, she's got a memory like a steel trap.

Amazing choice, too. She selected Duncan's "There's no art to find the mind's construction in the face." After my epic misinterpretation of her behavior on Monday, it's hard not to suspect that she was sending me a message about how *I'd* jumped to conclusions. The way she justified her choice of that line and the expression on her face as she spoke certainly added fuel to that speculation.

Part of me wishes I could take back the way I behaved toward her in my dad's office, but then again, something about that meeting seems to have changed the dynamic between us. I feel more relaxed when I see her in class and I definitely wasn't as wound up during today's tutorial as I was during the first few sessions.

I'm almost afraid to hope for it, but I think Aubrey and I are on the way to becoming "friends," which, despite my desire for more, is certainly a welcome and appropriate compromise. I won't deny that I'm still pained at the thought of her going home to Matt, but I suppose I've reconciled myself to the fact that she's off limits.

That didn't stop me from wanting to grin at her stupidly throughout the entire tutorial, nor did it keep me from praising her performance after class and asking about her plans for Reading Week. Just making conversation, right? Of course, what she doesn't know is that I was virtually taking notes as we talked. (She'll be staying in residence all week; she's not going away because she's saving for a summer trip to Europe; she looks ridiculously hot in the tight black sweater she wore today…)

I made small talk in return. What I didn't tell her, as much as I wanted to, was that with one word from her, I would cancel my plans to go to Ottawa in a heartbeat. In fact, I was sincerely tempted to invite her out for coffee during the week, under the guise of chatting about her independent study or something equally absurd. As much as I was aching to — I can't think of anything I'd rather do right now than sit down with her in a quiet café and talk for hours — I can't risk something like that. I doubt I'd make it through the encounter without becoming a rambling fool.

When we finally went our separate ways, I wished her a good week off, but what I really wanted to say was, "You have no idea how much I'll miss you…"

(I did just claim I've reconciled myself to the fact that she's off limits, right? I'm hilarious.)

Between hanging out with Penny and Jeremy, taking my parents to the airport on Saturday and picking them up today, and visiting Patty this afternoon, I've been fairly busy over the last few days. Busy is good. It keeps my brain occupied. But tonight, I can't sleep. My thoughts are racing and I need to clear my mind.

I've quite capably avoided thinking about my weekend in Ottawa, but now that the trip is three days away, it's become impossible to evade my own thoughts. When I picked my parents up from the airport this morning, they invited me over for a family dinner on Saturday. I declined, and told them I was going to Ottawa to visit Sabrina, but made it clear that friendship is ALL there is between us. In the process of saying those words, I convinced myself once and for all that I truly have no desire to rekindle anything with her.

I feel like a heel for opening this can of worms and possibly misrepresenting my intentions to Sabrina. My behavior is selfish and unfair. While trying to distract myself from my inappropriate thoughts about Aubrey, I'm hurting someone who's always been a good friend.

I was driving down Front Street after dropping off my parents, and all of this shit was swirling through my brain, when I *swear* I saw Aubrey crossing the road and going into the St. Lawrence market. Perhaps my mind was playing tricks because I was thinking about her, but I don't think so. I'd go as far as to say I'd know those amazing legs anywhere. I actually pulled over and contemplated running into the market to pick up something—anything—simply to have a chance of "bumping into her." In the end, I thought better of it. Wisely so, I'm sure. I can just see myself trying to make small talk with her while holding a coil of kielbasa sausage and a wedge of Emmentaler cheese. It's a scenario from a bad sitcom.

Needless to say, afterward, I couldn't stop thinking about her, and was still distracted and scattered when I arrived at Patty's for an afternoon visit. Patty was rather distracted herself. I found her in the dining room, listening to Frank Sinatra, with papers scattered everywhere. As it turns out, the papers were letters—love letters—all from Gramps. I assumed they were from their courtship, but Patty explained that he wrote them over the course of the year he was teaching her. He didn't give them to her as he wrote them—he couldn't. Instead, he parceled them together and gave them to her after she graduated. I knew Gramps was a charmer, but I never took him for such a romantic.

Patty gave me one of them to look at. I actually got a lump in my throat reading about his feelings for her and his hope that she would remain unattached until she graduated so he might have the opportunity to court her. He also spoke of the extra difficulty of breaking up with his fiancée, whom he said he knew wasn't right for him once he'd met Patty—"my darling Henrietta," as he called her.

In that letter, he quoted Browning's "A Face." I read the poem out loud to Patty and she chuckled (with a tear or two in her eye), and said, "Can you blame me for being completely smitten?" She told me their relationship may have been horribly complicated at first, but she wouldn't have traded a single minute of those months of uncertainty or the first messy weeks of their courtship for anything in the world. Then she disappeared into the bedroom and came back with a book of love letters by some of history's most renowned figures. Apparently, my grandfather was a notorious plagiarizer and even in his later years, he would write her letters and cheekily steal words from this book while trying to placate her after a transgression or argument.

She pressed the book into my hands, telling me she wanted me to have it, claiming that Gramps would have wanted his tradition continued. I told Patty I didn't have anyone to write love letters to, but she looked at me in that way she has—like she knows far more about what's going on in my heart than I do—and insisted I bring it home with me because you never know…

So here I sit, looking through the letters in this well-worn book that my grandfather leafed through and quoted from as he wooed my grandmother, apologized for a screw up, or tried to explain how much he missed her during a separation. I can't help thinking of all the letters he wrote during the school year while he and my grandmother secretly yearned for each other, just as I'm (albeit unrequitedly) pining for Aubrey. Our situations are nothing alike, but I find myself wanting to be hopeful. As Patty said…you never know.

And what would I say to Aubrey now if I were free to speak my mind? If, like Gramps, I could steal someone else's words and have them speak for me, what would I tell her? Well, I found a letter by Keats which is a little over the top…okay, it's REALLY over the top, but it does capture some of my frustration at not being able to spend time with her and get to know her:

"My Dearest Girl,

I have been a walk this morning with a book in my hand, but as usual I have been occupied with nothing but you: I wish I could say in an agreeable manner. I am tormented day and night… 'Tis certain I shall never recover if I am to be so long separate from you: yet with all this devotion to you I cannot persuade myself into any confidence of you…

You are to me an object intensely desirable — the air I breathe in a room empty of you is unhealthy. I am not the same to you — no — you can wait — you have a thousand activities — you can be happy without me. Any party, anything to fill up the day has been enough.

How have you pass'd this month? Who have you smil'd with? All this may seem savage in me. You do not feel as I do — you do not know what it is to love — one day you may — your time is not come….

J. Keats"

I keep re-reading that last line. *"One day you may."* There's hope in those words. (I'm choosing not to think about the details of Keats' ill-fated engagement to Fanny Brawne. I think I'll stick with my grandparents as inspiration…)

There's a line.

There is *always* a line.

I knew full-well where that line was and I crossed it. No, I didn't simply cross it. I got inebriated, stomped all over it, and THEN I crossed it.

I've often thought Romeo a simpering drip, but the words "I am fortune's fool" come to mind today. Ironic really, because I thought things were finally about to start going my way. Sabrina called early yesterday morning to tell me she had the flu and that she would have to cancel our weekend visit. She mentioned something about rescheduling when she felt better, but she didn't say anything specific. She didn't sound particularly coherent and I wasn't about to try to force the issue to firm up alternate plans. I made all the obligatory expressions of sympathy, and then hung up, feeling like a prisoner who's been granted a reprieve.

I certainly don't wish her ill, but I can't begin to express how relieved I was knowing I wouldn't have to see her this weekend. I don't know if that makes me a coward or an ass, but at that moment, I couldn't find it in myself to care. I felt as if the tides were turning in my favor. Then a giant wave came out of nowhere, picked me up and threw me against the rocks.

After frittering away my day of freedom, I impulsively decided to take my parents up on the dinner invitation they'd extended earlier in the week. I shaved, got dressed for dinner and made my way over to their place. When I arrived, my dad greeted me at the door, surprised to see me, but happy I was joining them because they had a guest joining the family—someone he's wanted me to meet for a while.

Well, of course, because my life consists of one insanely fucked up nightmare after another, the dinner guest happened to be none other than Aubrey Price. Let me see if I can remember how my dad described her: *bright, attractive, a lovely girl I'd have a lot in common with...*

In a nutshell, my dad was standing there, telling me he wanted to set me up with the very girl I've been tripping over myself to avoid thinking inappropriately about for the past few weeks. What in the ever living fuck? I mean, seriously?

I was forced to explain to my dad that I couldn't stay for dinner, and I CERTAINLY couldn't buddy up with his dinner guest because Aubrey is in Martin's class — in *my* class — and his plan to throw us together was completely out of the question! He lost it (understandably, I guess). My immediate reaction was to get the hell out of there, but it was too late. Mom intercepted us, dragged us into the front room, and then in walked Aubrey. She'd been in the powder room and had heard my *entire* exchange with my dad.

This is where the camera cuts to me, wishing the earth would swallow me whole. I sensed the most uncomfortable and embarrassing scene was about to unfold. After everything that happened last year, if my mother had known she was in the process of abetting my father as he tried to forge a match between me and one of Martin's students, she would have had a frigging nervous breakdown. But just as I was about to fall off the curb into the path of a speeding bus, Aubrey grabbed my arm and pulled me back to safety. While my father, either genuinely dumbstruck, or simply *playing* dumb, failed to reveal what he now knew, I feigned ignorance as well, pretending to be meeting Aubrey for the first time, and God bless her, she went right along with the charade, sparing us all an ugly scene.

Sure, it was only a matter of time before my mother would have to be told, but thank Christ, it didn't happen right there with the whole family in attendance. Mom and Dad sent us all off downstairs to enjoy ourselves before dinner, and I did what any hysterical man would do when, by awkward happenstance, he finds himself in the company of the beautiful young woman he wants most in the world but can't have. I started drinking myself into oblivion.

As one does.

It was the worst thing I could have done, but it felt like the only way to cope. I mean, there was Aubrey Price, perching her perfect ass on a bar stool in our basement where I've sat a million times, and she was just hanging out, drinking a beer, chatting with Penny and my brothers, laughing at their antics…it was one of those clichéd "pinch me" moments.

Things got progressively stranger as the evening wore on. One minute Penny was telling me she's met Aubrey before, on Valentine's Day in the washroom of Canoe of all places, because Aubrey was there the same night we were there, with Matt as her date (cue my absolute shock and jealous rage which I proceeded to wash down with a half pint of Guinness). Then Aubrey was profusely denying ANY romantic attachment between she and Matt, which seemed to give Penny the green light to play matchmaker for Aubrey and me, using healthy doses of her trademark innuendo and irreverent humor (zoom in to an extreme close-up of my red-faced quasi-adolescent fumbling discomfort chased down with the other half pint of Guinness).

As for dinner, it was a farce. Terror stricken, I was incapable of chewing my food. I don't think I ate a bite. Watching Aubrey field my mother's questions without batting an eyelash, all under the watchful eye of my dad, was truly amazing, though. The girl's unflappable. So while she was blithely navigating a Grant family dinner, I was drinking my face off. By the time we returned downstairs after dessert, I was feeling no pain whatsoever. That's when things got a little blurry.

Jeremy was in his own world, Penny and Brad were pawing each other like horny teenagers, and in the midst of this, I was tossing back countless beers and getting more and more uninhibited with every passing minute. I don't mean to use drinking as an excuse — there's no excuse for my behavior — but as much as I tried to keep my wits about me, I had the hardest time keeping my eyes off Aubrey, entranced by her every move. Each time she lifted her beer bottle to her mouth and wrapped her lips around the rim, I was possessed with an unrelenting need to touch her. It was pure agony. So I did the only thing I could under the circumstances. I offered to teach her to play snooker.

Obviously.

(This is the part of the evening where I decimated the "line" I was referring to earlier…)

The snooker "lesson" quickly went downhill. Inhibitions long abandoned and good judgment apparently out the window, I proceeded to launch into one thinly veiled innuendo after another. Then

I touched her—slid my fingers along her arm, wrapped my hand around hers, disguising my movements as an attempt to teach her how to hold the cue. I was lost. The next thing I knew, I had Aubrey bent over the table and was leaning over her back, pressing against her, all under the auspices of instructing her how to properly line up a shot.

I can't recall what I said or what she said in that moment (although I do know it was all quite sexually charged). I do remember Aubrey looking up at me over her shoulder—her eyes—God what she does to me with those eyes! How I refrained from throwing the pool cue across the room so I could do a variety of very dirty and wholly inappropriate things to her is beyond me.

Regardless, by that point, "the line" had been crossed irrevocably. I mean I was literally mashing my hard-on against her ass. Despite being overcome with lust, I was suddenly gripped by horror, as I realized (with a little help from Brad) that I was doing the *very thing* Nicola had accused me of. I was sexually harassing a student! I turned away as I quickly as I could and escaped upstairs. My mother and father quickly saw that I was borderline wasted and sprang into action, my dad resolving to take me home immediately.

Aubrey and I shared that ride home, but we didn't share any further words or glances. In fact, I have little to no recollection of the trip. I think I passed out within seconds of leaving my parents' driveway.

And now I sit here, utterly ashamed and not sure what to do next. Not that I haven't heard plenty of advice and suggestions. I've been on the phone on and off all day. Mom's appalled at the idea that she was "tricked" by Aubrey, someone she thought was quite lovely and who "seemed" so genuine and intelligent. I begged her not to blame Aubrey, trying to point out how trapped the poor girl was. Then I got an earful from my father—the usual. All completely predictable.

I spoke to Jeremy and Brad too, filling them in on all the behind the scenes shit. Though I didn't speak directly to Penny, I gather she's completely mortified at the thought that she was being so flippant about Aubrey all night, pushing us together, all the while ignorant of the fact that this was the girl I've been telling her about for three weeks. What a mess. They must all be shaking their heads in disbelief.

But I can't worry about my family right now. I'm more concerned about Aubrey. What must she think of me? In my booze induced haze, I suppose I was quite happy to assume she was being warm and flirtatious in response to my advances, but what if she felt as if she had to behave that way because of my relative authority? God, I can't face her in that classroom. I can't just waltz in and look at her as if nothing untoward happened. No, before even attempting to sit across from her in the lecture hall, I'll have to speak to her. Apologize somehow, for behaving so poorly…

On the other hand, Aubrey's no fool. From day one she hasn't shied away from disagreeing with me and standing up for herself. If she'd felt I was out of line, she would have made her disdain clear. Wouldn't she? Brad did tell me he thought she seemed perfectly at ease and quite happy to go along with what I was doing. Jeremy confirmed as much, saying he never would have guessed she was uncomfortable. Why shouldn't I lean toward their interpretation instead of assuming I'm doomed? Why am I so quick to assume the worst?

Because, as Shakespeare's Antony said, "All strange and terrible events are welcome, But comforts we despise," *that's* why.

My piss poor luck is never-ending.

And my penchant for hyperbole is verging on absurd.

If I could speak to my grandfather right now, eke out a kernel of advice about how to deal with the predicament I find myself in with Aubrey Price, he'd probably sigh deeply, pat my knee and comfort me with one of his favorite historical aphorisms. Perhaps he'd haul out, *"Kites rise highest against the wind, not with it."* This is wishful thinking. I can't imagine my grandfather encouraging me to buck the system where my most recent moral transgression is concerned.

I met with Aubrey today. I called Martin and told him I was ill and wouldn't be able to attend his lecture or conduct my tutorial. I waited for Aubrey after class and followed her to the Gardiner Museum where I caught up with her as she was browsing through the second floor ceramic displays. I interrupted her solitude after watching her for a few moments, and she turned, looking at me with those eyes — eyes that registered surprise, perhaps even shock. But then her expression softened, and I read relief in her gentle blink and hesitant downward glance, followed by encouragement in her sweet, warm smile.

If I'd thought I was merely going to apologize — tell her I was sorry, wash my hands of my antics on Saturday and then move on — my resolve disappeared instantly, my determination to do the right thing evaporating as I looked into her beautiful green eyes. Before I knew it, I was inviting her downstairs for a cup of coffee. She didn't give me a chance to regret the invitation, replying almost immediately with three wonderful words: "That sounds perfect."

At our table in the restaurant, I tried to stay on course. I apologized for my inappropriate behavior, for the way I'd talked to her and touched her on Saturday, but she seemed intent on treating the incident as a joke, saying she'd enjoyed our pool table encounter. I thought perhaps she was trying to spare my discomfort by letting me down easily. But when I pointed out that I was serious, she simply looked me dead in the eye and said, "So am I."

Done for.

Completely and utterly screwed.

What was I to do? She'd *enjoyed* my overtures. She hadn't been humoring me on Saturday, out of some fear of the power dynamic. She had welcomed my advances! The attraction I thought I'd imagined was real — as real for her as it is for me. What she'd claimed on Saturday is true, after all: Matt is nothing more than a roommate. Aubrey is at liberty to attach her affections to whomever she wishes. What she seemed to overlook this afternoon, and what I damn near forgot myself, were the epic ramifications of Aubrey attaching her affections to me.

I was at a crossroads. I could have told her I stood by my apology and that I regretted putting her in an uncomfortable position and that it wouldn't happen again, or…

(And this is where Gramps would frown from under his shaggy brows and shake his head.)

I didn't follow my grandfather's example. Instead, I took a huge leap of faith and told Aubrey exactly how I feel about her, and somehow, over the course of the next ten minutes, we went from being Daniel Grant, TA, and Aubrey Price, fourth-year student, to two people who obviously want to spend time together, to get to know one another, to be together…

I'm making it sound as if I don't understand how this new dynamic between us came about. But I do understand. There was a moment, so precise, so specific that I could distill it onto the head of a pin. You see, after I'd shared my feelings with Aubrey, I found myself apologizing — backpedaling, I suppose — telling her that I was aware of the inappropriateness of my overtures. She looked me straight in the eye and asked me if I'd think she was a horrible person for not caring if my feelings for her were wrong.

How did I refrain from knocking the table over, eliminating the stupid wooden impediment between us so I could pull her into my arms and kiss her senseless? Somehow, God knows how, I controlled this impulse, and this is where I take the moral high ground. Perhaps I shouldn't have told her how I feel. I shouldn't have intimated that I wanted to pursue a relationship with her one day, when the time is right. *But at least I restrained myself physically.* Frankly, I amaze myself.

Our fingertips met in the middle of the table. It was the briefest moment of connection, but at the same time, the most intimate of touches. A bond seemed to form between us in that instant. I almost heard something snap into place. It was as if I'd been trapped in a vault for a year and Aubrey had her ear pressed against the unlocking mechanism. Somehow only she could spin the lock and find that magical series of numbers which would allow the tumbler to click.

It clicked. I stepped out. And then I didn't know what to do with myself. What else was there to do but walk her home?

We strolled side by side, not touching, but occasionally looking at each other, both of us smiling (she beautifully, me ridiculously, I'm sure). We talked logistics. Nine weeks until semester's end. Nine weeks in which we'll have to keep a low profile and bide our time. I have no doubt this will be the longest nine weeks of my life.

I left her there, in the lobby of Jackman Hall, ostensibly to pick up my car and carry on with my day, all the while thinking, CAR? DAY? WHO THE FUCK CARES? But then as I was walking away, I found a glove on the sidewalk — might it have been hers? — a perfect excuse to double back. I did just that and found her curled up on the floor crying. God help me, my Aubrey was crying, and I was supposed to leave? She claimed to be overwhelmed by the events of the preceding hour.

(I could have told her that made two of us.)

I comforted her as best I could without compromising myself — as always, imagining cameras tracking my every move. This is what Nicola's false accusation and my paranoia have done to me. I suppose I fancy myself the star of a never-ending episode of Candid Camera, self-conscious in the extreme, aware of every public movement.

So yes, I walked away. I had to. It was the only way to save myself. If I'd stayed longer, I'm sure I would have pulled her into my arms and kissed her tears away. Then her tears would have stopped, and I would have kept kissing her because…because once I kiss her, I know that will become my sole purpose in life.

To kiss her as much and as often as possible.

Moments after leaving her in that vestibule, the predictable questions began to bubble in my brain. What had I done? What was I going to do now? The answer presented itself immediately. Have an anxiety attack, of course—not a full-blown attack, merely the early stages of one. This isn't surprising. I was probably in shock, completely taken aback by what I'd just done, throwing myself into the line of fire like that, giving Aubrey plenty of rope to hang me with, if she chose to use it. Could I be more self-destructive? The more I thought, the more confused I felt. Chatting with Penny and Jeremy over coffee afterward, attempting to justify my foolhardy actions to them, merely heightened my distress.

Oddly enough, a phone message from Martin upon my return to the condo late this afternoon reminded me that my frustration over not being able to pursue Aubrey freely and with unrestrained passion is actually not the most earth-shattering crisis imaginable. The death of a student has put my ridiculous "problem" into perspective. Having no luck reaching Martin to clarify the nature of the fatal incident he'd briefly alluded to in his message, and not even clear about the identity of the victim, I foolishly rushed back to Jackman, without an ounce of forethought, to make sure Aubrey was okay. Not knowing her apartment code, I had no way of gaining entry to the building, but I managed to sweet talk my way in with a couple of residents. After walking aimlessly up and down the second floor of Jackman, not entirely sure which apartment was Aubrey's, I finally heard her voice through one of the doors. Thankful that she was okay, although mildly disgruntled to hear her laughing and having a grand old time with Matt ("sweet cheeks," she calls him—I could cheerfully throttle him), I escaped from Jackman unseen and made my way home.

I eventually heard back from Martin, and sadly, Mary Langford is the student who died. She perished in a car accident last Wednesday.

It's times like this that I struggle against cynicism. Life is so frigging fragile. And it's in light of this complication that I wonder if maybe my grandfather would be easy on me—tell me to "live a little." I'd express my desire to do just that, but also share my frustration at not knowing what lies ahead, telling him how much easier things would be if we could know the future implications of our actions in the here and now. Gramps would quote Churchill and warn me to be ruled not just by my heart, but by my head.

Good old Churchill. Why couldn't he have been a flakey old romantic? How I wish he'd been famous for saying, *"Run to her, boy. Grab her tight and never let her go."*

I don't know what tomorrow holds, but tonight? Well, tonight I have to make a phone call. I must call Sabrina. I can't prolong the inevitable with her. We have no romantic future. I won't be looking to arrange an alternate weekend in Ottawa. This will not be a pleasant call. God willing, it will go smoothly.

(I've invoked God's assistance so many times today, I fear I may owe Him my right arm, or potentially, my first born. My parents would not be impressed with this sort of irreverence. My mother would be quick to point out that God is not Rumpelstiltskin.)

Time.

On the one hand, there's far too much of it, at least in the context of waiting. Fifty-eight days? Fifty-nine? Maybe even sixty…That's how long I have to wait until I can pursue a relationship with Aubrey. It seems an eternity. Already, I feel the measuring, the counting, the wishing away of hours and days will become an obsessive enterprise.

(How wonderful. I need some new obsessive tendencies.)

On the other hand, how can I be so self-absorbed? I'm blessed to have so much time lying before me, ready to unfold. Time is an unknown entity. How much time do I—or any of us, for that matter—have left? It's a frightening reality, and one that's so easily dismissed until something horrific like the passing of Mary Langford happens.

This is the essence of my dilemma. I'm torn between wanting to stroke the dates off a calendar with gusto, and knowing I need to savor every hour, appreciating the small gifts every new day affords. In light of this recent tragedy, I'm tempted to say, who has time to waste on dallying? If Aubrey and I want to be together, shouldn't we simply seize the day? With some careful planning and discretion, no one would have to know…

But every time thoughts like this creep into my brain, I squash them. This philosophy is self-serving and has potentially dangerous long-term consequences. And I know myself too well. Even if we were to make it through the next two months unscathed, I'd know that I had compromised my position and I would wallow in guilt. The idea of tainting our developing relationship that way is not an appealing one. (That doesn't mean I don't think about her all day long, though, desperate to spend time with her.)

Yesterday, I sought the grace of God and the wisdom of my grandfather. Today, I feel as if I need the strength of Hercules to resist the overwhelming need to see Aubrey and then control the surge of physical desire that rocks me whenever I'm with her.

I had no logical cause to park myself outside Old Vic at one o'clock this afternoon. Yet where did I find myself at one o'clock this afternoon? Why, right outside Old Vic, of course, all in the hope of catching a quick glimpse of Aubrey. (Thank fuck I documented our early encounters. A quick read-through reminded me that we'd crossed paths in the quad on a Tuesday several weeks ago after I'd had a late lunch with my father. She'd dashed into Old Vic, most likely to attend a one o'clock lecture. There's something to be said for the obsessive recording of minutia, after all.)

While I stood there, debating whether she'd show up, I also found myself wondering what she'd think if she did cross the quad and find me standing there. Would she be freaked out by the fact that, for the second time in as many days, I'd magically appeared before her out of thin air? And I can't help but wonder, had she truly been prepared to wait until Wednesday's class to see me? If so, how much more ridiculous would I feel, pining for a glimpse of her — anything to sustain me until our next scheduled in-class meeting?

My concerns were unfounded. For one thing, Aubrey *did* appear in the quad at the appropriate time, and she didn't take issue with me knowing she would be there. Most importantly, she seemed just as happy to see me as I was to see her, leaping at my suggestion that we spend some time together after her French lecture, using a meeting about her independent study as a pretext. I was left whiling away two hours as she sat through her class.

I found myself at Chapters, suddenly inspired by a pile of calendars on the discount table. I had a recollection of myself as a boy, counting down the days to Christmas on the calendar in my room. One year in particular stands out in my mind. We were going to the cottage for Christmas, and Brad, J and I had requested a train set from Santa — one of those massive ones that takes over a whole room. By Hallowe'en, all three of us were counting the number of "sleeps" left until the big day. The excitement of that countdown was almost as delicious as the prospect of the gift.

Standing at that table in Chapters, staring at the calendars and thinking about Aubrey, I felt the same sense of expectation. I picked up two identical calendars with Shakespeare's likeness on the front cover, one for each of us, thinking, *let the countdown begin*. It will be a painful wait, but somehow, I can't help thinking that the anticipation will be worthwhile. In this age of instant gratification and entitlement, how often do we have to postpone the fulfillment of our wishes? I'm not saying this is going to be easy—not by any means. If Aubrey weren't so beautiful and witty and warm and fun (and yes, sexy as hell…) perhaps it wouldn't be so difficult, but in the space of an hour today, she made me laugh more than I have in the last few months altogether, and aroused a rather painful physical reaction on more than one occasion.

After I'd told her about Mary—news which understandably upset her, and made me wish I could pull her into my arms and console her—we retreated to the E.J. Pratt library. We chatted, and giggled like a couple of fourteen-year-olds on a first date, disturbing many other library patrons in the process.

She called me "sailor." Odd choice of nickname, but every time she said it, I felt this strange proprietary buzz. *This is my girlfriend,* I thought, fully aware of the puerile nature of the term, but reveling in it, regardless. *This my girlfriend's affectionate nickname for me.* We rubbed knees, we shared silly anecdotes about the first time we saw each other. She told me she'd had a dream about me after the first day of class. I gather it was a rather steamy one. How bizarre it is to look back now and reevaluate our first meetings with this new understanding, knowing she was just as intrigued by me as I was by her.

The highlight of our rendezvous (and this is the epitome of absurdity, but must be taken in context) was hugging her under the Gatehouse archway. Ridiculous, no? I could tell myself it was just an innocent embrace, but it wasn't. I clung to her, my heart pounding as I felt her hands slide around my neck and into my hair. I breathed in her essence, felt her lips against my neck. I wanted to cradle her head there and beg her to kiss me. It would have been so easy to push her into the dark corner…

I did not. I collected myself. I stepped away. We shared our frustration. (Oddly enough this shared frustration took the shape of a line or two from *The Winter's Tale*…) But even after expressing my irritation with the situation we find ourselves in, I was still a bundle of contradictions, and felt incapable of clearly articulating my feelings to her, not even sure if I should try.

Now, it's midnight, and my thoughts continue to whirl every which way. How will I ever sleep? I keep telling myself that sitting down and writing will help clarify my thoughts and calm my mind. It's not working. When I try to distil my thoughts into cogent, straightforward prose, I see Aubrey in my mind's eye, and everything seems to go slightly out of focus. It's not an entirely unpleasant sensation. I would liken it to reaching for a pair of reading glasses and picking up a prism instead. You wouldn't be able to read a newspaper through it, but you'd be treated to a beautiful array of light and color, all the same…

WEDNESDAY, MARCH 4

t's been a long day, one I wasn't even remotely rested enough to face. Perhaps my exhaustion is to blame for my outlandish behavior. I'm not sure how best to justify it, but I wish I could take back my actions.

Having secured an alternate venue for my Friday tutorials after class today, I should have headed to the English office to check on my office hour appointments before my meeting with my advisor, but once again, I was drawn to Aubrey, and since I'd heard her telling Julie she was going to the Hart House library to do some reading, I felt compelled to swing by, hoping to share a few words with her. Plus, I had a note burning a hole in my pocket, something I wanted to give her which I'd penned late last night after reading poetry until all hours. I thought she'd find a handwritten note romantic and charming. Somehow, I doubt that's the final impression I left her with after our encounter today.

When I arrived at the library, she was flaked out on a couch reading. I sat in a chair across the room and watched her for a while. Every few pages, she'd look up and stare into space. She seemed so melancholy…wistful almost…so beautiful. At one point, she stood and looked out the window for a few moments. Sadly, she was wearing a really long sweater. Happily, I have a fertile imagination. I swear, the thought of her luscious ass in those tight, black pants makes me lose the ability to think rationally.

A few minutes later, rational behavior joined its counterpart rational thought—both having gone up in smoke, apparently—and the next thing I knew, I was texting her (revealing my presence in the room and again feeling like a bit of a stalker, for the third day in a row) and begging her to remove her sweater. Whether this was a playful request or a desperate command, I don't know, but Aubrey complied, regardless. She unbuttoned and slipped off the sweater and, perhaps understanding the motive behind my words, she returned to the window, taunting me by stretching her hands over her head. In addition to affording me a chance to salivate over her glorious ass, this move gave me a quick glance at a swath of creamy skin below the hem of her T-shirt that begged to be touched and kissed.

The way she looked at me over her shoulder as she slowly lowered her arms made me utterly unravel.

Was she more sensuous today than other days? Was there something about the quiet tension in the room that inspired my quickening desire? Or had Tuesday's meeting—the embrace we'd shared, the feeling of her breath on my neck, her fingers in my hair—had this promise of physical delights to come awakened an insatiable lust that had to be articulated? I don't know. I can't account for what I said and did next.

I pictured her on that sofa with sunlight streaming across her naked body. I saw her beckon me to join her, begging me to kiss her, and even though this was all a fabrication, the machinations of my overwrought imagination, I needed her to know how much I wanted that—how desperately I wanted to devour her lips with mine, and then traverse her entire body with my tongue. The physical need to do this was acute to the point of pain.

I sent her a series of pointed and wildly inappropriate text messages, the physical gestures accompanying them undeniable in their intent. If she were ever to recoil, fearful of my feelings and the passion inspiring them, today would have been the day. She didn't. She met my eyes. The desire in her gaze matched my own. Had we been alone in that room, I would have seduced her on that sofa without another thought. It stands to follow, then, that I owe my safe escape to the handful of undergrads sprawled around the room. After drawing Aubrey's attention to the note I was leaving for her on the chair, I fled, taking a moment to send her a plea from the hallway, begging her to erase our ill-advised correspondence. Good sense had returned, and with it, the potential peril of having put my lewd desires into words became clear.

Given the raunchiness of the exchange I'd initiated, I'm sure she was expecting the note I'd left behind to be similar in nature. It wasn't. It was quite lovely, actually, inspired by the Bard's wonderful words in Sonnet 57.

"Being your slave, what should I do but tend
Upon the hours and times of your desire?
I have no precious time at all to spend,
Nor services to do, till you require.
Nor dare I chide the world-without-end hour
Whilst I, my sovereign, watch the clock for you,
Nor think the bitterness of absence sour
When you have bid your servant once adieu;
Nor dare I question with my jealous thought
Where you may be, or your affairs suppose,
But, like a sad slave, stay and think of nought
Save, where you are how happy you make those.
So true a fool is love that in your will,
Though you do any thing, he thinks no ill."

- W. Shakespeare

Could I have picked a poem whose tone was more incongruous with the behavior I'd just exhibited? Aubrey must think I'm mad. I may well be. With fifty-seven days in the interim, by the end of the semester, I could be positively certifiable.

"Whatever."

I hate that word. I never hear it without wanting to throttle the person saying it.

What does it mean?

Do whatever you want. It makes no difference to me. I don't care. Fuck you.

If I'd ever doubted the damage words can do, Nicola made their catastrophic powers clear with three words. Those three words that she uttered — *he molested me* — they didn't just damage my life, they obliterated my hopes and dreams. Indeed, I'm no stranger to the power of words.

And last night, Aubrey dealt me a "whatever." I lost my shit.

I have no idea how it happened. Everything seemed fine on Friday. We went to Mary's service, not a happy occasion by any stretch of the imagination, but we were there for each other, our fingers secretly intertwined during the whole ceremony. I felt so grounded by that simple touch. It's amazing how quickly I've grown to rely on Aubrey as a stabilizing force. She validated this feeling in a note she gave me afterward in which she mentioned that she feels connected to me, even when we're apart. I was heartened to see how in sync our feelings were. It seemed to further underscore our compatibility.

Desperate to forge ahead, eager to know everything about her, to understand what makes her tick, I convinced her to meet me at the Four Seasons Hotel after the service. We shared a clandestine embrace in the stairwell, and feeling her in my arms, so soft and warm, her body melded to mine, I was reminded of the slippery slope I was navigating, revisiting the anguished journey of my week and recalling the advice Penny had shared over breakfast that morning. "Just get it over with," she'd said, claiming I've already lost my objectivity and might as well follow my instincts with Aubrey.

I refused to see that as my only option, believing it entirely possible to nurture a friendship with Aubrey. Certainly affection would come into play, but I reasoned that there was no need for either one of us to give in to primal sexual urges. I was convinced that we could move forward with a chaste courtship in which the primary goal was simply getting to know one another.

With that philosophy in mind, I talked Aubrey into joining me for lunch at the Four Seasons, and we spent two hours enjoying a leisurely meal, during which we finally had a chance to talk — properly. I have to admit, there were a few suggestive moments, but we seemed to navigate our way through the minefield of desire and stay remarkably focused on learning about each other. In fact, over the course of those two hours, we covered a hell of a lot of ground.

I discovered that her parents are not only divorced, but they've both relocated, leaving Aubrey here in Toronto to fend for herself, something she's obviously doing quite admirably, working part-time and still managing to carry a full-course load while achieving Honors standing. Listening to her talk, I got a very clear sense of her pride and determination. Knowing the obstacles she's overcome made me feel ashamed of the lack of financial obstacles I've had to face. For as long as I can remember, I've been surrounded by luxuries and all manner of indulgences.

Despite the many things Aubrey and I have in common (not the least of which is our mutual fondness for witty repartee and an affection for Elizabethan literature), we've had very different upbringings. I find myself wanting to give her everything — to take her to nice restaurants, to buy her clothes, to take her on trips...in short, I want to spoil her silly. Already I can tell that won't be easy. Have I mentioned she's stubborn as a fucking mule?

Have I also mentioned she's so sexy she can liquefy my bones (all but one of them), with a simple hug, a few suggestive whispers and a coy glance from under her eyelashes? The embrace we shared in the underground car park as we headed to my car was very nearly pornographic, despite the fact that we were both fully clothed and we didn't even so much as kiss...

Essentially, when faced with her charms, I become a dithering idiot. I've swung from one extreme to the other and back again (several times) this week—horny and desperate one minute and restrained and prudent the next, back and forth, changing my tune with the direction of the shifting wind. I suppose it's no wonder things fell apart last night.

The day started well enough. Aubrey and I talked on the phone (yes, I took the plunge and made first contact). We had what amounted to a very normal phone call between two people who have just started dating. We even had the most hilarious "phone sex" exchange, innocent enough, and primarily in jest, but another reminder of not just her fantastic sense of humor, but of exciting things to come.

At least that's what I thought yesterday. Now I'm not so sure of our future. We went to the benefit concert in honor of Mary last night, had a great time with my brothers, Penny and Julie, and as far as I was concerned, it was a successful evening. Sure it was a little tense here and there, with Cara's arrival, and Matt's unfortunate presence (he's like a bad rash), but having Jeremy, Brad, Penny, and Julie around us, finally aware of what's going on, normalized things.

Maybe that was part of the problem. Perhaps that's what inspired Aubrey's uncharacteristic outburst last night in the taxi. It was bad enough that I climbed into the backseat of that car with her in the first place, but then to find myself in a position where she was kissing my neck, whispering in my ear, pleading with me to bring her home to the condo…well, how was I supposed to react? She seemed to have lost her ability to think straight and completely forgotten the inadvisability of us being alone together.

But when I tried to talk sense to her and remind her of the precariousness of the situation, she snapped. I tried to reason with her, but by that point she was too angry to listen. She simply crossed her arms and shut down. I decided she needed a chance to cool down and think things through. As we pulled up to the condo, I asked her if it would be okay if I phoned her, and that's when she delivered those three unfortunate syllables:

What-ev-er.

In light of that "whatever," I didn't call Aubrey today. At first, I couldn't bring myself to phone her because I was angry, but the more I think about the situation, the more I realize I'm partly to blame for what happened. All week, I've sent her mixed messages. I can't expect to go from being suggestive and playful, verging on seducing her and then suddenly pull back, do a complete 180, and claim surprise at her reaction.

Now I'm avoiding calling because I'm actually afraid of what she might say. What if she's decided this whole mess is too much aggravation? What if I'm the only one who's an emotional train wreck right now? And that's not as inconceivable as it might seem. I called Penny to tell her what had happened and discovered that she'd called Aubrey to chat and that Aubrey sounded fine.

Fine?

She sounded *fine*. What the fuck?

So here I am analyzing every detail of our argument and trying to figure out what to do next, and Aubrey's fine? Am I over reacting? Did I imagine her hostility? I don't think I did. Perhaps she was putting on a brave face for Penny, knowing Penny would talk to me. I can imagine Aubrey doing that. Not that I blame her — I see myself doing exactly the same thing. Excessive pride is something else we have in common and it's not hard to hide your feelings over the phone.

But what if pride has nothing to do with it at all? What if she *is* perfectly fine? Fuck, this is painful. How did my grandfather do it? Over seven months he waited, hoping against hope that Patty would still be available to him at the end of the school year. The man must have had nerves of steel. I'm not sure I have it in me. To be honest, I find myself re-evaluating my priorities. I wonder how hard it would be to get a transfer to another course section. As much as I'm enjoying Martin's class, as well as the course content and the students I'm working with, perhaps it would be a good idea to explore my options. Hell, maybe I'm not ready to be a TA at all!

Between now and tomorrow, I have to do a great deal of thinking. And since I'm so completely ignorant of Aubrey's state of mind, I'll have to proceed cautiously (especially if I hope to preserve my own damn pride).

It seems to me that regardless of what I decide to do, there will be an inherent sacrifice.

Sacrifice. Not a fun word. Almost as unpleasant as *whatever*.

MONDAY, MARCH 9

It's seven a.m. and I'm about to head off to U of T. I'm grabbing coffee with my dad at eight, but I'm going to go to the interoffice mail depot first, to drop off a parcel for Aubrey. Yes, I'm making the first move. Perhaps I've read too many stories in which the main character is destroyed by his own hubris. Having said that, I'm also wary of allowing myself to show weakness. I don't know how much my heart can take.

I bought Aubrey new gloves yesterday afternoon — a goodwill gesture, restitution of a sort for losing her gloves on Saturday. I'm also enclosing my black T-shirt in the parcel. Aubrey said that if she couldn't have me in bed with her, she would at least like some item of my clothing to sleep in. If she reads between the lines, she'll understand the significance of me giving her the shirt.

I've been sitting at my desk for an hour now, carefully composing a note to enclose in the package. I think I've finally found the right balance of disappointment, contrition and regret tempered by a small dose of cautious hopefulness. I've written, deleted and rewritten, agonizing over every fucking word. At this point, I have to trust that the important words will speak for themselves —

We need to talk. I was careless. I'm sorry. Your choice.

All that's left now is to deliver the parcel and see what comes of it. Once it's in her hands, there'll be no going back.

THURSDAY, MARCH 12

In the space of three days, everything has changed. I won't pretend to understand Aubrey and her motivations. I can only imagine she found our relationship too restrictive. Like she said on Saturday, she doesn't have a lot of patience. The waiting was obviously too unappealing.

When I saw her on Monday, I truly thought there was a chance for us to patch things up. She was cool toward me at first, but then she acknowledged my gifts, and seemed to soften. We managed to have a civil conversation. I suggested we get together to hash everything out in person and she agreed. We had a bit of trouble finding a time that would work for us both, but we finally settled on Tuesday night. She was to have dinner with Julie at the Madison House, and I would pick her up at 8:30 so that we could go somewhere and talk.

My first mistake was arriving early. My second mistake was going inside the Maddy to collect her. Julie wasn't there at all. Instead, I found Aubrey locked in an intimate embrace with Matt Miller. I did the only thing I felt I could do in that moment: I turned tail and ran. The rest is sordid, pathetic, post break-up history. I came home, almost had another panic attack, got drunk, woke up on Wednesday and puked my guts out, and then I went to class. Aubrey was absent. Thank Christ.

Looking back over the week, I know I haven't handled things well. I've received a few random texts from Aubrey, wanting to "explain." I'm not ready to hear her excuses, not quite prepared to have my nose rubbed in my inadequacy. No doubt she thinks I should have stayed at the Madison on Tuesday and taken my defeat as a man. Well, there's no way that was happening. If I'd stayed, an ugly scene would have ensued. I imagine it would have looked something like this:

Me: Well, Aubrey, now I understand what you meant the other night. Thanks for clearing up my confusion.

Aubrey: What do you mean?

Me: When you said "whatever"? Obviously you meant, "sure you can call, but I might be going at it with my so-called roommate."

Matt Miller: Dude, why don't you fuck off? You can see the lady's not interested.

(This is the part where my fist makes contact with his face.)

Random bar patrons: Aubrey, why is your TA beating the shit out of your roommate-slash-boyfriend?

Aubrey: Oh, you know, he's a bit of a head case. Definitely a loose cannon.

My dad: I told you something like this would happen, Daniel, but you didn't listen…

My father was not at the Madison. I have no idea how he made his way into this imaginary tableau. I guess he must be talking to me from his perch on my left shoulder. Fuck, I need a drink. Yeah, I know drinking won't help.

Whatever.

What makes a kiss so incredible? What exactly is it about the pressing together of lips and the warm mingling of tongues that drives me so wild? I've always been a sucker for a woman who knows how to kiss, but when it's Aubrey's lips and tongue in question, how the FUCK am I supposed to restrain myself?

Yes, my whole world has been flipped on its ass. Yesterday was a life-changing day for me, and I'm not saying that to be dramatic (for once). I think the actions I took yesterday quite literally altered my fate, and Aubrey's too, because if I hadn't done what I did, she might be well on her way to dating someone else right now, and I'm hazarding a guess that someone else is Shawn Ward. (Although I can't be sure, I've seen the way he's been looking at her lately and I don't like it…)

I'd like to claim responsibility for the wisdom of my actions this evening—would love to give myself a congratulatory pat on the back for swallowing my pride and finally comprehending the consequences of my cowardice, but I can't. I owe my reconciliation with Aubrey almost entirely to Matt Miller. Yes, I'm talking about the person I could have cheerfully strangled several times over the last few weeks. Now I'm considering sending the guy a fucking fruit basket.

He made a special trip to confront me earlier today after a tutorial that may well have been one of the most mind bogglingly frustrating hours of my life. Aubrey was an absolute firecracker, and while I wanted to shake some sense into her during the tutorial, I can see in retrospect that I'm the one who needed a good tooth-rattling shake. At the time, oblivious to the truth, I thought she was being irrationally supercilious, but now I realize her contempt was well-founded.

Matt, obviously aware that Aubrey and I have feelings for one another, trekked across campus to put me straight, informing me of my misplaced anger and wildly inappropriate accusations. What I saw on Tuesday night was not a lovers' embrace after all, but Aubrey physically propping up a drunk and despondent Matt for fear that he might fall flat on his face.

In short, I jumped to conclusions and refused to contemplate that there might be an explanation for what I saw, other than infidelity. The question that reared its ugly head, of course, was "why?" Why was it so easy for me to assume Aubrey was being deceitful? The only answer I could conceive of is that it was convenient. No man relishes betrayal, and I'm certainly no exception. However, for me, inherent in this supposed betrayal was an escape clause—an opportunity to weasel my way out of a relationship which was forcing me to behave unscrupulously and making me consider a course of action I hatched last Sunday, but clearly didn't want to pursue: the voluntary switching of courses, or the complete abandonment of my Teaching Assistant position for the semester.

These options were both distasteful. The fact that I avoided bringing the subject up with Martin, even after I'd decided on the solution, proves that I didn't want to broach the topic. Thinking Aubrey unfaithful was an easy out, making me, quite plainly, a coward. Of course, I didn't connect the dots all week, not comprehending that *I* was the one pushing *her* away, and not the other way around. I did a stellar job of alienating her, but I didn't understand how successful I was in my efforts until Matt explained that Aubrey was prepared to move on, and that someone seemed to be hovering in the wings waiting for her to be ready. The final nail in the coffin came when I looked in the bag Julie gave me after tutorial. When I found the gloves, T-shirt, and calendar I'd given Aubrey, I knew she meant business.

Somehow, seeing this ACTUAL evidence of her desire to wash her hands of me, brought me face to face with the truth: I couldn't bear to lose her, and if she turned her back on me for good, I'd have no one but myself to blame for having destroyed the fragile connection we'd forged in the preceding weeks.

That's why it seems impossible to me that no more than two hours ago, after talking at length, we managed to patch things up. Not only did I humble myself by taking full responsibility for our misunderstanding, I also shared with her the story of what happened at Oxford last year. Initially, my reason for telling her was to give her greater insight into my struggles with impropriety and to perhaps justify my wildly swinging moods. But also, what better way to prove to Aubrey that I know I was wrong to question her integrity this week than to entrust her with my deepest secret?

There was an instant during my confession when I thought she might be doubting my claim that I didn't behave at all inappropriately with Nicola—after all, what was I to think when she said to me, "Did you molest that girl, Daniel?" But when I vociferously denied any wrongdoing, Aubrey looked at me with an expression of the deepest compassion and said, "I had to ask. I thought you might like to see what it feels like to be asked the question by someone who'd believe your answer unequivocally." Is it any surprise then, that I've given myself over entirely to the stirrings of my heart?

Moments later, we found ourselves dancing together (at the Palais Royale, no less) and drinking champagne. And now I sit here remembering not just the feel of her body pressed against mine, but the taste of her lips, because yes, at last I took the plunge: I finally stole a kiss—though to say I stole this kiss would imply an unwillingness on Aubrey's part, and in light of her passionate response to my advances, it's fair to say she was an enthusiastic participant. Now our first kiss is branded on my tongue, and it's truly sealed my fate. There's no going back now.

That divine kiss paved the way for the most amazing good night embrace (which is probably best described as a make-out session), during which I ached to touch her and I couldn't restrain myself. I caressed her leg, slipped my fingers under her dress and teased at the edge of her stockings, mere inches away from paradise. All this happened in the front seat of my car. We were like a couple of teenagers with no place to go, and I suppose, in truth, there is nowhere safe for us. On campus, we're at the mercy of prying eyes; at my condo, I'd be a danger to both of us, incapable of controlling myself.

(Although how I wish I could put that claim to the test. The thought of spending the night with her in my arms is driving me wild.)

Her delicious lips and soft skin will be my ruination. She knows how desperately I want her. I couldn't resist telling her at last, whispering my deepest desires, just as I'd wanted to do that night four weeks ago today, in the dark of the Hart House theater. I'm a throbbing mess just thinking about the way her warm thighs parted under my touch and the feel of her breathy sighs against my neck....

Fuck...I can't torture myself like this anymore. The only safe place for me now is the shower...

SATURDAY, MARCH 14

I've never considered myself a flake, prone to believing in lucky charms or talismans, spirits or sixth senses. This evening, I might be convinced to revise that world view. I would have been tempted to consider yesterday's fortuitous turn of events a fluke if it weren't for the fact that Matt Miller was so clearly the mastermind behind my reconciliation with Aubrey. But what happened to me this afternoon, I can't dismiss as coincidence, especially when coupled with something Aubrey said last night.

The morning passed ordinarily enough. I dropped by my parents' place for breakfast and mom gave me some plants to drop off at Penny and Brad's. I delivered the plants and helped Brad move some heavy pieces of furniture around. While I was there, I took a few moments to call Aubrey, so grateful for the return of the easy banter we'd been starting to enjoy before things fell apart last week. I confirmed our dinner plans at Patty's for tomorrow, and we left things at that.

I felt good, relieved at the reconciliation and looking forward to taking her to Patty's. I know my grandmother is going to like her, and it goes without saying that Aubrey will think Patty's great. Even so, driving home from Penny and Brad's and still thinking ahead to tomorrow evening's dinner, an uneasiness began to brew in my mind. Perhaps thinking about Patty was stirring up thoughts of my grandfather, making me question what he would think now that I've truly crossed the line with Aubrey.

So I turned around, and instead of going home, I drove out to High Park to sit on my grandfather's bench, something I haven't done in quite a while. I don't know if I thought going there would clear my head, or make me feel closer to him and therefore help me to get a handle on what he'd think. I honestly don't remember because what ended up happening was so strange, it wiped out all recollection of rational motivations.

I sat there mumbling away to my grandfather as I'm so prone to doing when I sit on his bench. I told him about Aubrey, said I wished he could have met her and given me his blessing, and then I confessed that I worried he might be disappointed in me for behaving so unscrupulously. My rambling was interrupted by a woman who was walking her Black Lab — or more aptly, I was interrupted by the Lab dragging the woman toward the bench. The dog jumped around excitedly, sniffing at me and wagging its tail maniacally, all but grabbing my leg and humping me.

The woman was embarrassed and apologetic, explaining that she's been walking Lucky in High Park for years, and when the dog was young, an elderly couple would often be sitting on the bench on Sundays, and the gentleman was always enthused to see the dog, petting him and fussing over him, eventually always seeming to have a treat at the ready for his arrival. So now, Lucky still looks for the couple whenever he and his owner pass the bench. Of course, I immediately assumed she was referring to my grandparents, and when I described them to her and explained that my grandfather passed away a few years ago, she confirmed that it did seem as if Lucky's pal and Gramps are one and the same.

That alone was enough to make me feel closer to my grandfather, but then the woman sat beside me and told me she'd often stopped to chat with my grandparents and, thanks to their talks, she's gone back to school and is finishing a History and Classics degree at York University after being out of school for fifteen years. Then she pulled a small, well-thumbed paperback from her coat pocket — the collected works of Petronius, one of her current readings.

Of course, I congratulated her on her new found commitment to learning and told her my grandfather would be proud. She smiled sadly and said she knew he would, confessing that she had a feeling he'd be quizzing her weekly about what she was studying and what she'd learned. At that moment, I didn't just feel my grandfather's presence, I felt the responsibility of his influence on this woman's life, and inquired how her reading of Petronius was going. She laughed, as if she knew I was trying to fill in for him. She told me she's halfway through *Satyricon*, but that it's one of the poems from the second half of the book, one of only a few remaining poems attributed to Petronius, that she's actually become attached to.

(This is where things get a little weird.)

She gave me the book and I read the poem, not once, but twice, unable to believe my eyes, truly believing that my grandfather was communicating with me through this woman, her dog, and this ratty paperback book. (I swear I'm stone-cold sober now, and was three hours ago when this incident occurred.)

The poem seemed to echo something Aubrey said last night, when she told me she wanted to start at the beginning and not at the end — that having a chaste courtship wasn't such a bad idea after all because we'll have time to get to know one another without the complications of sex. I agreed that this was a sound line of thinking. After all, it's what I've been arguing all along. We renewed our pact to avoid physical overtures, knowing that even casual dating is still a trespass in the eyes of the university, regardless of how much we restrain our passion. Of course, no more than an hour later, things fell apart with the sharing of our first kiss and several very intimate touches. It's this backward slide, initiated by me, that I've been berating myself for.

But then I read the poem, and my first instinct was to take it as a sign. Given the way in which I stumbled upon it, I can't help associating it with my grandfather. I must include it here, for I'm sure I'll be referring to it often…

"Doing, a filthy pleasure is, and short;
And done, we straight repent us of the sport:
Let us not then rush blindly on unto it,
Like lustful beasts, that only know to do it:
For lust will languish, and that heat decay.
But thus, thus, keeping endless holiday,
Let us together closely lie and kiss,
There is no labour, nor no shame in this;
This hath pleased, doth please, and long will please; never
Can this decay, but is beginning ever."
~ Gaius Petronius

This poem echoes almost exactly what Aubrey said last night about taking things slowly. That alone comforts me, but this claim is even more reassuring: *"Let us together closely lie and kiss, there is no labour, nor no shame in this, this…is beginning ever."* What an amazing validation of the situation Aubrey and I find ourselves in. No shame? How much I want to believe that!

Maybe it's convenient for me to see this as a sign, but if feeling as though my grandfather's hand is at work here helps me come to terms with the turn of events, then so be it. I can't pretend that my attraction to Aubrey is entirely virtuous—I'm a man, and she's beautiful and sexy and incredibly enticing. But I'm deciding here and now that I'm going to stop beating myself up for the way things have progressed.

Life is too short. Aubrey is right. While we're counting down, instead of being annoyed by the need to wait, we should enjoy the time and truly get to know one another. A few kisses here and there aren't the end of the frigging world.

One day, I might tell Aubrey about the events of this afternoon, but not yet. She's liable to think I'm a head case. All that matters is that I'm at peace with the way things stand. With approximately six weeks in the interim, Aubrey and I will continue to enjoy connecting intellectually, our hearts will grow closer the more time we spend together, and then, our physical union will merely be a logical next step.

There is no shame in wanting to fall in love with the person I desire before sharing complete physical intimacy. I can say, without a single reservation, that this is not about wanting sexual release or a quick hook-up. When we can finally be together, I'll be making love to Aubrey, and considering the fact that she can knock me on my ass with a look and make my knees buckle with a single kiss, I know I have so much to look forward to.

Part Three

Love Letters

MONDAY, MARCH 16

Hi, beautiful,

I'm testing the waters here, dipping my toe in, I suppose. I've recently discovered that my grandfather wrote to my grandmother before they were able to be together—numerous letters proclaiming his affection for her. Somehow, he knew one day he would share those letters with Patty. When I first found out about the letters I was in awe of his faith. Before this weekend, I'm not sure I could have said with any certainty that you and I will still be together in May, having successfully endured the constraints of the TA/student relationship.

I'm certain now. Everything has changed. And why that change? Quite simply because I woke up with you in my arms this morning. I know without a shadow of a doubt that I want to share my heart with you. I wish I could pour out my feelings to you, but I dare not. Like my grandfather, I need to proceed with caution. And so, as an homage to him—or perhaps to the love he and my grandmother shared—I'm going to give this letter writing (or in my case, letter *typing*) a try.

Last night was incredible. I honestly think we've found a way to navigate the complexities of our relationship, both individually, and as a couple, but more than that, after resolving our conflict from last week, I think we respect and understand each other better. Do you know where the final vote of confidence came from, though? From Patty herself.

I'm not sure if you realize how important it was for me to have my grandmother's approval when I introduced you to her. I lived in England for so long, and made so many decisions without the advice or influence of my family, I forgot how wonderful it feels to have their support. With things being so tense between me and my parents, Patty's endorsement means so much. You made a great first impression last night, Aubrey, and trust me when I say Patty is an excellent judge of character.

When she launched into the story about how she met my grandfather, and you saw the way their story parallels ours, you must have thought she was psychic. Not once did I tell her how we'd met, and that you were a student in Martin's class. How did she know we would benefit from hearing her tale, a story that ended so happily?

Well, there's a very logical explanation.

I visited my grandmother a few weeks ago, and when was showing me my grandfather's love letters, she made a reference to the "complicated" way her courtship with my grandfather had started. Last night when we were at the table, and I described our relationship using the same word, she obviously knew exactly what I meant. Of course, she didn't judge. She understands our predicament perfectly.

She's lived it.

Something else you don't know, and which I dare not tell you now, is that after dinner last night, when you went to the washroom, Patty showed me an engagement ring, the one my grandfather gave her when he initially proposed. He bought her a new ring on their fifth anniversary, but Patty has always kept her first ring. Last night she told me she wants me to have it, and one day, when I'm ready, she wants me to use the diamond in the ring I give to "the woman I choose to share my life with." She didn't use your name, but why else would she have shown it to me last night, if not to suggest that I hold on to you?

She put her hand on my cheek, told me to breathe, and counseled me to live entirely in every moment you and I spend together. Last night I did my best to follow her advice.

By writing you these letters, I'm going to try to record those special moments so I can share them with you later, instead of simply ranting and venting to nothingness. I hope that's okay with you, and I also hope that when you read these letters one day (because I'm determined you will), you'll appreciate the feelings inspiring them and not simply think me a soppy sod.

(That's a Penny-ism. You may need to consult her for a translation.)

I tried to put Patty's advice into action as soon as we left her house last night. I was afraid to admit this to you because I'm sure you'd have thought me a complete head case, but when I took you to my grandfather's bench, I was introducing you to him. Having felt his presence so acutely the day before, visiting his bench again was the best I could think of to do by way of introduction. I sensed his approval and wanted so fiercely to hold on to that moment. My peace of mind was palpable. I think that's why I asked you to spend the night with me. I could see the interminable weeks stretching before us, but all I could think about was *now*.

Let Browning explain what I seem to be at a loss to articulate…

"Out of your whole life give but a moment!
All of your life that has gone before,
All to come after it — so you ignore,
So you make perfect the present, — condense,
In a rapture of rage, for perfection's endowment,
Thought and feeling and soul and sense —
Merged in a moment which give me at last
You around me for once, you beneath me, above me —
Me — sure that despite of time future, time past, —
This tick of your life-time's one moment you love me!
How long such suspension may linger? Ah, Sweet —
The moment eternal — just that and no more —
When ecstasy's utmost we clutch at the core
While cheeks burn, arms open, eyes shut and lips meet!"
~Robert Browning

That sums up how I felt last night, Aubrey — my simple but burning need to obliterate the rest of the world and cling to you, holding on to *that moment* in time — the way I feel when you kiss me.

I realize things got away from me once we were back here at the condo. I should have known how incredible it would be to hold you in my arms, safe within these four walls, without fear of prying eyes. Lying with you on the couch, feeling your body pressed against mine…quite frankly, I lost myself. What started as "a moment" became an all-encompassing desire. What I feel for you is so much more than just a physical impulse, but my God, the need to make love to you — to show you in some tangible way how I feel about you? Disregarding this need is becoming more difficult to manage with every passing day.

That's why I've written everything down for weeks. Catharsis is essential to the analytical soul. I often wonder what you'd have thought if you'd opened these files on the flash drive last night. Would the enormity of my feelings and the volume of words I've spilled about you have scared the crap out of you? Perhaps I'm underestimating your feelings. We both skirted the issue last night, and the "definitely-maybes" are fun to bandy around, but for me, there's no maybe about it, Aubrey. Perhaps I can't tell you to your face yet, but I can tell you here without fear of scaring you away: I'm falling in love with you. Realizing this fact has me terrified and euphoric in equal parts.

(Most terrifying are the logistical implications. These are the questions I ask myself: How do I impartially evaluate the essay of the woman I'm falling in love with? How do I call you *Miss Price* during tutorial, and not *sweetheart*? How do I walk away from the classroom without leaning over to kiss your forehead and say, "I love you, poppet—I'll call you later…")

You see my dilemma. As complicated as I'm making my existence, though, I can't imagine any alternative now. Talking to you on the phone this evening was one of the best hours of my day, although it couldn't eclipse waking up with you lying beside me (or should I say lying on top of me?!). And how can I forget the events that followed this morning?—seeing your beautiful bare legs and those sexy black panties for the first time (sweet torture), sharing morning coffee with you (pure contentment), standing between your creamy, white thighs while you watched me shave (agonizing delight)…

I've already relived the events of the past twenty-four hours a hundred times—several times during class today. Do you realize how happy it made me to see you walk into the room wearing the LV gloves I bought you? I'm glad you lost that silly striped glove! Of course, then I had to spend an hour watching you biting your lip, remembering the taste of your kisses and the way it feels when you draw my lower lip between your teeth…

Fuck, the distance between us torments me, but knowing you'll be staying over again on Friday, having something tangible to look forward to in four days, the forty-five day wait between now and May doesn't seem so insurmountable.

As for now, it's approaching midnight. My eyes are burning and I really should sleep. If sleep won't come easily, I'll stare into the darkness and conjure up images of your warm responsive body beneath mine, your eyes softly closed as your lips, sweet and eager, meet mine again and again…

If thinking about me affords you even one-tenth of the pleasure I experience when I think about you, then you're a happy girl, indeed.

Yours,

(With not a single "maybe" in sight),

~Daniel

xoxoxo…

WEDNESDAY, MARCH 18

I miss you, Aubrey. God, how I miss you. Missing you makes me do crazy things. You're probably going to kill me, but I've booked us a night at Taboo, a resort up north. It's in the Muskokas, far away from U of T and the potential scrutiny we have to endure here. I'm excited as hell, and I hope you'll be excited too. We can leave as soon as tutorial is over on Friday. (*Please* be as happy about this as I am…)

I fear when I tell you, you'll pull out the voice of reason, and I suppose you have every right to play Devil's advocate, laying out the dangers of going away together. I promise, it's not my intention to spirit you away from the city to seduce you (although when I read over what I've said and thought for the last few days that seems impossible to believe…). I simply want to relax and have some fun with you—to go skiing, to go for a walk outside, in broad daylight, holding your hand without having to worry about who might be watching. Doesn't that sound wonderful?

How strange this is—talking to you as if you'll be providing an immediate answer and knowing you won't. Actually, this is the most bizarre situation I've ever found myself in. I'm sure I've never experienced so many emotional highs and lows in such a short span of time, nor thought so deliberately about my experiences. I often berate myself for this overindulgence in analysis, but then today, reading a book of love letters Patty gave me, I saw over and over again, this same tendency to self-examination. Gustave Flaubert flagellated himself daily for his manic self-analysis, but it's the words of John Keats that I always return to. I can almost hear myself in his words…

"My Mind has been the most discontented and restless one that ever was put into a body too small for it. I never felt my Mind repose upon anything with complete and undistracted enjoyment - upon no person

but you. When you are in the room my thoughts never fly out of window: you always concentrate my whole senses." (1820)

See what I mean? What great company my discontented and restless mind is in! I can't thank my grandmother enough for giving me this book. It's becoming my bible. Any thought or feeling I doubt or call into question is validated tenfold in the pages of this book, by history's greatest thinkers, no less!

I open my eyes every day, tortured by thoughts of you and counting the minutes until I'll see you again, scoffing at my obsessive thoughts, but what do you know?—even Napoleon, the great military and political leader fell prey to the joys of amorous connection and the misery of the separation that follows. His anguished letters to Josephine litter the pages of this book:

"I have been very dull ever since we parted. I am happy only when with you. I never cease thinking of your kisses, your tears, and your amusing little jealousies: the charms of the matchless Josephine ever keep my heart and feelings warm…I believe I have always loved you, but I think I love you a thousand times better now than ever…" (1796)

Oh, Napoleon, you poor sod! I understand his preoccupations, Aubrey. It's only been a little over forty-eight hours since our lips met, and I'm so, so ready to feel you in my arms again. However, I must somehow banish these ardent thoughts and put on my game face. See you on campus in an hour, my gorgeous girl. I can't wait.

Faithfully yours,

~D

xoxoxo…

Good morning, poppet,

I've again woken up at an ungodly hour. It's five past six, and I can't get back to sleep. I'm positively vibrating with excitement. (Wanna rub up against me? ;)

I'm so glad you've agreed to our getaway to Taboo. I confess, it was tense there for a few moments yesterday when I told you about the weekend I've planned. I thought you were going to refuse me. But hallelujah, you agreed, and you even accepted the gift card and went shopping at Holt's. This is progress!

I know I should feel trepidation about taking you away, or at least a trace of guilt, imagining what people would think of me if they knew what I was doing, but somehow I don't. The only person's judgment I fear is yours. You are the only critic whose words can affect me now. You told me last week you aren't terribly familiar with Shakespeare's sonnets. Here's one for you which sums things up perfectly:

Sonnet 112

"Your love and pity doth the impression fill,
Which vulgar scandal stamp'd upon my brow;
For what care I who calls me well or ill,
So you o'er-green my bad, my good allow?
You are my all-the-world, and I must strive
To know my shames and praises from your tongue;
None else to me, nor I to none alive,
That my steel'd sense or changes right or wrong.
In so profound abysm I throw all care
Of others' voices, that my adder's sense
To critic and to flatterer stopped are.

Mark how with my neglect I do dispense:
You are so strongly in my purpose bred,
That all the world besides methinks are dead."

I need you to understand this, Aubrey. You have to know how important you are to me—that you're "my all-the-world." You know what? Screw it. I'm going to email you. I realize it's yet another leap of faith, but what better way to prove my feelings for you than to entrust you with my words?

I'll leave this letter here. When next you hear from me, I'll be introducing you to my alter-ego, Jung Willman. He leans toward histrionics from time to time, but you'll get used to him. I happen to think he's a rather endearing chap.

See you soon, and in case you're at all unsure, I can't frigging wait to kiss you again. I'm also very excited about seeing you in skis. I'm in dire need of a good belly laugh. ;)

Love,

~D

xoxoxo…

MONDAY, MARCH 23

Hello, my love,

Before I say anything else, I have to apologize again, Aubrey. I'm sorry for abandoning you on Friday. For not telling you about my anxiety weeks ago. For turning to my mother in the office on Friday instead of reaching out to you. For our lost weekend and all the fun we could have had. For the promises you've had to make to my father. For my past, and for all the compromises my baggage is foisting upon you—upon us. And on and on it goes…I'm so sorry.

All of this seems too much for someone to tolerate, and yet there you are, putting on a brave face and enduring everything. I asked you to forgive me this morning, and you told me there was nothing to forgive, as always, the epitome of understanding. I suppose I had no control over the events of this weekend, but I still feel horrible for essentially deserting you here, not knowing what was going on.

My dad told me about the conversation you two had the other day—how you said losing gloves is your tragic flaw and he told you he's never heard of one of Shakespeare's heroes spiraling to his downfall because of a lost glove. The irony is rich, isn't it? Think of all the chaos that's unraveled, all because of that stupid striped glove. Regardless of the cause, there's no turning back. We can't erase what happened. Now we must try to move forward.

I won't pretend I'm happy about the arrangement you've made with my father. I guess I should take comfort in knowing things could be much worse—at least it was my father who found us out and not someone else. Being forced to drastically rein in our behavior doesn't change what's in my heart, though. I'm not prepared to apologize for my feelings. I'm not sorry we met, and I'm not sorry

I'm falling in love with you—HAVE fallen in love with you. I won't apologize for wanting to be with you every minute of the day, for wanting to talk to you and laugh with you, for wishing I could hold you and kiss you…

It's inconceivable to me that we'll be completely out of contact, except for classroom time, without even texts or emails to sustain us, especially when I remember how excited I was to receive that first email from you last Friday. I suppose I'll have to reread it until I've committed it to memory, and fill this flash drive with even more letters to you that I'm not able to send.

All I can hope for now is that the coming weeks will pass quickly and without further incident. I'm notorious for torturing myself with recriminations and for overthinking everything, but I hope the wait and the time apart doesn't take too much of a toll on you. I would gladly bear the entire burden if it meant peace of mind for you, and that's the reason I'm agreeing to your conditions. I want your conscience to remain clear. I would hate to put pressure on you, heaping guilt on you in the process, so I will take my lead from you.

If I could make one demand of the universe, it would be this—

Sonnet 19

"Devouring Time, blunt thou the lion's paws,
And make the earth devour her own sweet brood;
Pluck the keen teeth from the fierce tiger's jaws,
And burn the long-lived phoenix in her blood;
Make glad and sorry seasons as thou fleets,
And do whate'er thou wilt, swift-footed Time,
To the wide world and all her fading sweets;
But I forbid thee one most heinous crime:
O, carve not with thy hours my love's fair brow,
Nor draw no lines there with thine antique pen;
Him in thy course untainted do allow
Yet, do thy worst, old Time: despite thy wrong."

Regardless of Shakespeare's intentions when he wrote this sonnet, my sweet, what I see within those lines is a desperate lover pondering the damaging effects of the slow passing of time while waiting helplessly for the day when he can be with the one he loves. Please don't allow the waiting to eat away at you. When you think of me and of our future, please anticipate the joy ahead of us and smile. I will try to do the same.

I hope you took my advice and gave the sonnets a read. I'm not sure how Shakespeare was able to tap into human nature with such facility, but for me, the sonnets are a treatise on the human condition, especially in dark times. In a couple of weeks, you'll be doing a sonnet analysis, which will bring us together, alone in a room, with the legitimate purpose of working through your analysis together. Is it entirely ridiculous of me to say I'm living for that meeting?

When I say things like that, I realize that my life has taken on the absurd qualities of an after-school teen drama, or perhaps a Kafka novel. I don't know which is worse. This weekend was particularly Kafka-esque, but despite the frustration I endured during the two days I spent up at the cottage, there was one positive outcome: inspiration. On Friday night, as I sat alone in the great room thinking of you, imagining you there with me (almost feeling your presence), I decided that we'll celebrate the end of the semester at the cottage. I'll make love to you for the first time in front of the fire, the light from the flames casting dancing patterns across your lovely skin, with my fingers following the journey of those shadowy flickers, enticing flames of their own.

God, I've done it again. Look how easily I get myself worked up! There are certainly drawbacks to having such a vivid imagination. (What would you say if you saw the evidence of what my overwrought imagination cooked up on Friday night? I'd better hope no one rummages through the desk drawer in my room at the cottage. They'd soon see substantiated — in rather unfortunate prose — the effects of having our weekend trip snatched away from me at the last minute.)

Well, I must close here. I have a whole set of tests to mark. I also have some messages on my phone that need attending to. I'll mark first. I fear listening to those messages you sent me over the weekend would entirely obliterate all hopes of productivity and merely send me straight to Jackman to pull you into my arms and hold you close for hours.

I remain most determinedly yours,

Daniel

xoxoxo…

Good afternoon, my darling girl,

It's a little after 4:30, and I've just received the most amazing email from you (and swiftly replied, of course…). When I emailed you last night after retrieving those messages from the weekend, I sincerely didn't mean to put pressure on you to respond. After reading and listening to your anguished words, I simply couldn't imagine not letting you know again how sorry I am for the way the weekend played out.

Hearing those messages made me feel sick. Imagining you thought I was capable of just ignoring you all weekend, of disregarding your calls and texts to meet some personal agenda gutted me. But then I realized, I have to take responsibility for you drawing that conclusion. I did do that to you a couple of weeks ago, when you reached out to me to try to explain what happened at the Maddy. I let my pride to dictate my actions. Allow me to assure you now: that will never happen again.

I said I didn't expect you to reply to my email yesterday, I meant it. I'd have been disappointed if you hadn't replied, but I don't think even I could have predicted how elated I'd feel upon receiving a response. Please don't think yourself a bad person. I agree wholeheartedly with your assessment: if communicating in writing will help you keep your promise to my father and ensure we don't both lose our minds in the meantime, then this is a good thing.

Right, I must be off. I have some book shopping to do. A certain young lady I know is in dire need of a pick-me-up and I think I know just the book that might do it. Hope you're having a lovely afternoon. I miss you. I'll write more soon.

(These letters feel even weirder now that we ARE communicating in writing, but I'm determined to finish what I started. I told you I'm stubborn. Persistent even. Compulsive…?)

Yours,

Daniel

xoxoxo…

Hi, gorgeous,

It's Friday—the end of another week, a really long week. The hours seem to stretch on interminably, don't they? It was so difficult walking away from you today. I confess I've never enjoyed a tutorial so much in my life. Lame, right? I'm glad Shawn pressed me to explain my views on love at first sight. I meant what I said. I truly think it's possible to recognize, from the outset, the essential qualities that you admire and appreciate in someone, in your case, qualities which go well beyond physical attraction. Romeo's first assessment of Juliet is certainly based on her beauty, but when I first saw you, Aubrey, the pull was so much more than a simple reaction to your physical attributes.

I saw this plucky girl, sticking her neck out when no one else would. The look in your eyes as you gazed across the room at me—defiance? A challenge? I don't know what it was, but there was such strength of character in your expression. I knew you'd be a force to be reckoned with (if only I'd had a clue just how powerful a force you really are…LOL). But then you blushed and lowered your eyes. Intelligence, strength and vulnerability, all in the space of a minute and a half—so compelling. Then I noticed your warmth and enthusiasm when you greeted Julie, and of course you stood up to hug her, and you were all long legs and tight jeans, beautiful shiny hair, fair skin, ruby red lips…and I was all asdfghjkl…(that's my brain being turned to mush…)

To put it succinctly, I was done-for in about two minutes flat. Well done, my beautiful, brilliant girl.

Thinking about your delicious lips quickly led to much more passionate (and much less appropriate) thoughts. I can't allow myself to feel too guilty about this. After all, history is replete with men who've fallen prey to the allure of an intelligent woman's beauty...

MY DOWNFALL

"My downfall: those pink articulate lips
Divinely flavoured portals to a mouth
Where soul dissolves...eyes darting
Beneath black brows, snares for the heart,
And the milk-white breasts, well-shaped,
The twin rosebuds, fair beyond other flowers."

Dioskorides wrote that in the third century BC, and millions of men have experienced the same downfall in the interim, I'm sure. That alone allows me to forgive myself for suffering a similar fate.

I'm serious when I call you "brilliant," by the way. Your brilliance actually got me into some hot water this week. I had the worst time marking your test the other night. It was perfect—every argument cogent and well-rounded, every example precise and spot on. How the hell did you do that, in the state of mind you must have been in on Friday? You boggle my mind, sweetheart.

Anyway, afraid to give you a perfect score, I took off a couple of marks for what might have passed for faulty logic (to a reader from Mars, who has no knowledge of the English language or Shakespeare's canon...I'm such a dick). Martin took exception to my assessment and gave me a talking to this afternoon. (Luckily, I was taking marks off, and not inflating the mark, so he couldn't accuse me of favoritism...) Simply put, my assessment was unfair (I put the "ass" in "unfair assessment"), and he's awarded you a perfect score. I'm pleased that he gave you those marks back, and particularly happy that it was his call to make, and not mine.

The incident has raised a red flag, though, not regarding my treatment of you, in particular, but about the need for clear assessment criteria. I'm sure we'll be working more closely on this for the rest of the semester, and frankly, I'm so relieved. That's another one of those issues my father's been harping on about since day one, so now I can say with all confidence, that our relationship won't affect your grades, one way or the other.

On that happy note, I'm going to have to sign off. I'm meeting Jeremy for a quick beer and giving him a book I've bought you. I'm hoping he can convince Julie to swing by your place and drop it off for you. I know how much you love Sarah Waters' writing, and in my humble opinion, it's a crying shame not to being able to buy yourself books because your budget is so tight.

Though I'm not with you, I feel the invisible thread that you read about in another one of Waters' books, strong as always, holding us together. Do you still feel it, Aubrey? That thread? I think it gets stronger every day, along with my affection for you.

Yours, heart and soul,

Daniel

xoxoxo...

Well, hello, my stubborn and incredibly sexy girl. Allow me to spend a few moments justifying that dichotomous description.

Stubborn: Don't you understand how much I love surprising you? I want to spoil you silly.

THAT is why I'm so frustrated by this arbitrarily imposed moratorium on gifts. Why must you be so stubborn? WHY?

I wanted to shake you today when you told me I'm not allowed to buy you anything for 31 days. Why can't you see the pleasure it gives me? You drive me crazy, you realize that, right? Is it not bad enough that I can't show my affection for you physically? I mean, look at the lengths I had to go to today to cajole you into spending ten minutes with me within a legitimate framework. I'm sorry you were upset by the way the grading of your test played out, but I won't apologize for seizing that opportunity to talk with you alone in the reading room — to hold your hand for five minutes and exchange a few quiet, intimate words.

It's beyond frustrating knowing I'm not just incapable of showing you affection with hugs and kisses, but now, I'm also hobbled by your ridiculous no-gifts rule. However, being the semantics aficionado that I am, I distinctly remember you saying, "Stop buying me things." That doesn't mean I can't GIVE you things. It only means I'm not allowed to spend money. This, my lovely, is what is often referred to as a loophole. It's also a challenge. And in case you didn't know by now, I fucking love a challenge. (And I'm just as stubborn as you are.)

Sexy: While our chat in the library was easily the best ten minutes of my day, I confess the discussion left me a little shaken. I never imagined we'd meander so off course as to find ourselves discussing blow jobs and your need to relieve your own sexual tension — WHICH YOU DID LAST NIGHT!?!?! God, what my imagination does with thoughts like those.

Speaking of which — my jeans, right now? WAY too tight. (I've realized that these are possibly the strangest love letters ever written, but I'm in too far to stop now. Just humor me, okay?)

I'll write again soon, poppet, but for now, I must go. I have some free gift brainstorming to do.

And other…stuff.

~Daniel

xoxoxo…

Hi, sweetheart,

It's late — I've just returned home from the first of three performances of *Much Ado About Nothing* at Hart House. Sitting in that theater with Julie beside me stirred up so many memories of February 13th, the night we sat together and watched *Hamlet*. Or at least some of *Hamlet*, because of course, then you threw up and I took you home and had to watch Matt swoop in like Prince Charming and take care of you, leaving me on the curb like a chump. God, such great memories! :)

I look forward to having you by my side again for the *Much Ado* performance. Between class, tutorial and the play, I'll be able to spend almost five hours with you on Friday! I'm particularly interested to see your response to the tutorial content. I know the sonnets aren't your forte, but once you get into reading them, I'm sure you'll agree they're lovely. This is one that I plan to share on Friday. It's my favorite:

Sonnet 116

"Let me not to the marriage of true minds
Admit impediments. Love is not love
Which alters when it alteration finds,
Or bends with the remover to remove:
O no! it is an ever-fixed mark
That looks on tempests and is never shaken;
It is the star to every wandering bark,
Whose worth's unknown, although his height be taken.
Love's not Time's fool, though rosy lips and cheeks
Within his bending sickle's compass come:
Love alters not with his brief hours and weeks,

But bears it out even to the edge of doom.
If this be error and upon me proved,
I never writ, nor no man ever loved. "

I've always loved that sonnet, but reading it now, I obviously think of our relationship and the obstacles we've encountered in the two months we've known each other. We've already overcome so much, and I feel like we can face anything. (Not that I'm looking to have to endure much more!) So when I read that in tutorial, I'll be legitimately covering course material, but I hope you'll realize as well, that I'll be reading it for you — *to* you.

I'm going to sign off now, as I have some mp3s to look through. I can't tell you why. It's a surprise. I'm certain it's one you'll like. Counting the hours until Friday, Aubrey.

Yours,

~Daniel

xoxoxo…

P.S. I just realized that when I flip open the calendar tonight, I'll be putting a big red X through the first day of April! Good-bye, March, and don't let the door hit your ass on the way out!

P.P.S. May 1st. One month today. Good God, make the time fly by!

Hi, my lovely,

The weekend has arrived. I've always looked forward to weekends, but not at the moment. Weekends separate us and that is not something I would ever wish for. Instead, I live for Monday, Wednesday, and Friday.

Yesterday was wonderful. I love watching your expression as Martin is lecturing. You get the most intense look on your face. Your kindness, wit, beauty and sexiness are all compelling as hell, Aubrey, but I really love your brain, too. You know that, right? I'd be hard-pressed to find someone more ideally suited for me than you are. (Shakespeare would call us *true minds*. I honestly believe that.)

As for tutorial, well, that was highly amusing. Watching you and Julie bashing knees under the table was very entertaining. You're so transparent sometimes. But just so you know, if Neil was my BFF, I'd have been giggling and bashing knees with him as well...) I would have said Shawn instead of Neil, but I'd like to bash something other than Shawn's knee, to be perfectly honest. Why does he remind me of a dog circling a T-bone steak when he looks at you? Don't think I didn't notice how excited he was to sit beside you at the show last night. It's so incredibly annoying knowing you're mine and yet not being able to announce it to the world.

I think the hardest part of this whole thing is that normally if I saw a guy salivating over you, I'd think, "Yeah, get an eyeful, buddy, but she's coming home with me." Somehow, thinking, "Go ahead, look if you must. She'll be coming home with me...NEXT MONTH" doesn't have the same ring to it.

Okay, I'm going to close here because I want to email you so that I can actually hear back from you. You see, that's the weird thing about writing these letters. Although I thoroughly enjoy the process, the lack of response is disheartening. Every time I sign one, I'm tempted to send the whole bundle off to you, but I stop myself. Like my grandfather did, I have to wait for the perfect time. With several weeks left in the semester, now is definitely not the perfect time. (Cue: Me already starting to obsess about the perfect time to give you these letters. I'm such an ass.)

Affectionately,

(The ass who adores you)

~Daniel

xoxoxo…

Hello there, green-eyes,

It feels like forever since I've sat down to write a letter, when in reality, it's only been four days. I suppose with time creeping by the way it is, every day seems endless. I would have written a word here and there throughout the week if I'd had time, but between classes and tutorials and the sonnet conferences I've been doing, I haven't had many free moments. The few quiet minutes I have had I've been using in other "creative pursuits," as you know, since you now have in your hands the CD and liner notes I painstakingly prepared for you.

I suppose I should thank you instead of cursing you for imposing the ban on gifts because it's forced me to think of other ways to show you my feelings, and I never thought I'd derive so much enjoyment from making someone a CD. The expression "labor of love" comes to mind.

To be honest, the hardest part of making that CD was narrowing down the playlist to thirteen songs. I would have included one or two more, but I'm developing a bit of a fascination with the number thirteen. If the events of February thirteenth and March thirteenth weren't enough, there's your birth date to underscore the magnificence of the number. So yes, thirteen is my new favorite number. (If you haven't already realized it, I have a tendency to be a smidge compulsive at times. Now, apparently, in addition to my laundry list of other foibles, I've become numerically obsessive. Awesome.)

Bottom line, I hope you like the CD as much as I enjoyed putting it together for you. I thought you would have listened to it by now, and I might have heard from you, but I suspect you might have fallen into bed as soon as you got home from your night class. You've had a taxing day, and just because I was the one conducting your sonnet conference, I'm sure that didn't make the assessment any easier. In fact, it may well have been more stressful for you. I was fairly nervous myself, but I tried to stay calm and completely focused to help you.

Stupid as it sounds, I loved reading that exchange from *Romeo and Juliet* with you and listening to your analysis. You did a nice job working your way through the themes and motifs, and I'm happy to have helped shed light on another possible angle of interpretation. You looked a little shell-shocked when I came out to give you your notes. I hope you didn't think you screwed up, because you did beautifully. I could have happily sat and chatted about the play with you for the rest of the evening. I've never had a romantic relationship with someone who shared my love of Renaissance literature before. I wish we had more time to indulge in long discussions about what we've read and enjoyed. One day…

Well, it's late, and I have more conferences starting at nine in the morning so I'd best turn in. As always, I'm thinking of you, and my heart is heavy as I contemplate the week ahead. I'll go to sleep tonight remembering the way you looked today as you read Juliet's lines. Just so you know, YOU kiss by the book. And I'm not referring to rules, convention, and propriety. I'm referring to my Achilles' heel, which I'm sad to report, is completely healed. I look forward to being completely crippled in a few weeks.

Good night, my sweetheart. I'll write more soon.

~Daniel

I sit down to write this evening, Aubrey, not having crossed paths with you today and without any hope of seeing you until next Wednesday. The thought is depressing beyond measure. At a time when you'll be alone, with no family to rally around you for Easter, I feel more than ever the need to be there for you—to support you and offer you solace and company, but heaven knows I could be in a room full of people, as I will be on Sunday, and still feel your absence acutely.

I've been so tempted to suggest that we find a time to get together during the next few days, somewhere safe and neutral, just to give us both something to look forward to over this very long weekend. I hope you think of me as much as I think of you because if you don't, then I'll feel even more foolish when I give you this collection of correspondence. Of course, there's always the book of love letters to turn to when I need a reminder that I'm not alone in my pathetic devotion to the woman I adore. For instance, look at this passage by Henry VIII as he pined for Anne Boleyn…

"…absence gives enough, and more than I ever thought could be felt. This brings to my mind a fact in astronomy, which is, that the further the poles are from the sun, notwithstanding, the more scorching is the heat. Thus is it with our love; absence has placed distance between us.

Nevertheless fervor increases—at least on my part. I hope the same from you, assuring you that in my case the anguish of absence is so great that it would be intolerable were it not for the firm hope I have of your indissoluble affection towards me."

Can you hear his agony? Were it not for the fact that Henry VIII was a violent and narcissistic asshat, I might actually sympathize with him. I can empathize with his plight, though. The absence of you in my days is painful. I know it's not your fault that we can't see each other, and I admire your strength, but that doesn't make the prospect of being apart from you for the next five days any easier.

Now I *know* it's a good thing I'm not sharing these letters with you. The last thing you need is me making you feel guilty for the decisions you're making—decisions which are good and sound and based on promises made to my father. Your determination to remain faithful to that promise to my father is staggering. And frustrating. (Infuriating is another word that comes to mind…) I should be grateful for your strength, but a part of me wishes you'd buckle. (It's quite a big part of me, actually. Can you guess which part it is?) ;)

I shouldn't write more. I'm not in the best frame of mind. I'm trying too hard. I hope to wake up tomorrow feeling less despondent. I think I'll devote my writing time this weekend to communicating with you properly, so I'm sure my letter writing here will cease for a few days. I hope you're prepared to hear from me every hour on the hour until I see you again. Brace yourself for an onslaught of drivel.

~Daniel

xoxoxo…

Hi, sweetheart,

How are you faring, my lovely? By now you'll have received my mother's care package and hopefully had a chance to enjoy dinner. Isn't Patty's pie amazing? And I hope you like the picture I gave you. I apologize for the rambling, nonsensical note I enclosed. I've been a wreck all weekend, to be honest, but I had to make some contribution to the package, since I clearly had nothing to do with the cooking.

You should have seen my mom, Patty, and Penny putting that parcel together in the kitchen while Brad and Jeremy kept my dad busy in the living room. It's safe to say that my mother is just as eager as we are for the semester to be over (well, maybe not QUITE as eager as we are…). She was saddened by the thought of you spending Easter alone and looks forward to the time when you can join us for family gatherings. She doesn't want you to hate her. I assured her that wasn't the case. (I hope that's not the case…) It was good of Penny and Brad to drop the package off for you. I told Penn to give you a hug for me. I hope she delivered.

Okay, poppet, I won't write more here. I think I'll email you now instead. I'm in dire need of some good-night words from you.

Talk to you soon,

~Daniel

xoxoxo…

Hi, my beautiful girl,

I'm still reeling from our afternoon visit. It was so unexpected, but so wonderful to see you. I don't want to waste time writing about Cara and the foolishness that prompted your visit in the first place. It was a horrible misunderstanding, and I can only hope that you'll never feel as if you have to keep something so important from me again. I didn't realize my anxiety issues frightened you so much, but rest assured, I'm accustomed to talking myself down. Don't ever avoid telling me something because you think I might get upset. I'll be fine. As for your concerns about Cara, I understand your worries, but I think I have that situation well in hand.

But enough of that. There are far more important things I want to think about. I can't articulate how wonderful it felt to finally to tell you that I love you. I'm sure there can't have been a single doubt in your mind about my feelings for you, but speaking those words? I feel entirely liberated. And have you any idea how comforting it was to hear you say you love me, too? There aren't adequate adjectives to describe how happy I am right now. Spending time with you this afternoon was an amazing bonus, especially since I thought I wouldn't see you again until Wednesday!

I know it sounds ridiculous, but our separations always plant seeds of doubt in my mind, allowing fears to run rampant in my heart. An afternoon with you in my arms—an hour of your kisses, your touch, your sweet words—has filled my heart and wiped out my despair, leaving me feeling whole again. Thank you so much for the lovely gift. I look forward to listening to the CD when you have the notes ready to share. I don't know what else to say, other than thank you, and I love you—so much—I wish I could properly explain how much. As Mistress Ford told her Falstaff, *"Heaven knows how I love you; and you shall one day find it."* Or perhaps I'll steal Walter Bagehot's idea. He once said in a letter to his wife Eliza that he was at a loss for words and thought he might simply write in big letters I LOVE YOU all the way across the page to emphasize his feelings. Let's try that out, shall we?

I LOVE YOU I LOVE YOU I LOVE YOU I LOVE YOU I LOVE YOU I LOVE YOU I LOVE YOU I LOVE YOU I LOVE YOU…!

Yes, that sums it up quite nicely.

Childishly and unequivocally yours,

~Daniel

xoxoxo…

P.S. I LOVE YOU!

Hey there, gorgeous,

Do you want to know the worst thing about being your TA? Aside from the obvious frustrations, of course, I hate that there are things I simply can't talk to you about because sharing them with you would constitute a conflict of interest. I know you're worried as hell about Cara and what she's discovered, and you're right to suspect that she knows exactly what's going on with us. After my meeting with her yesterday, there's no doubt in my mind that she's known all semester. The good news is I can virtually guarantee that she won't utter a word.

Unfortunately, I can't tell you why. It remains to be seen if I'll ever share what's transpired between me and Cara. All I can hope is that my assurances are appeasing you, and that you're not wasting time worrying about a situation that I have total control over.

I won't pretend that my handling of this little crisis has been "pretty." In fact, I feel kind of sick about it. I can't quite put my finger on why, but I'm sure it has a great deal to do with the implications of her blabbing. I'm doing my best to stay positive, however, and focusing my energies on the many things I have to accomplish this week, not the least of which is these *Much Ado* papers.

I marked a handful of them after dinner, and then out of nowhere, I was struck by blinding inspiration and dropped everything to work on my thesis. I'm not absolutely certain that anything I wrote made sense, especially given the inconsistent way I've been approaching my paper lately, but God, it felt good to lose myself in my writing for a couple of hours.

As I sat here working this evening, I came to a realization. You know what I'm really looking forward to? Seeing you sitting across from me on the sofa while I work at my desk. I know having you here will be distracting, but I can't help feeling as if your presence will also be so soothing and restorative, that I'll happily welcome the occasional distraction. How wonderful to set myself a goal and work away for a couple of hours, knowing that once I've finished, we'll be able to kick back and have a drink together, listen to some music, watch a movie, cuddle, neck for hours—

(I don't know what I'm talking about…I can't imagine be able to simply neck with you for hours. Five minutes of your kisses and I'm desperate to rip your clothes off…)

Anyway, that's beside the point. What I mean to say is that I can't wait to have you here with me (preferably permanently). You will be my muse, and I'll become prolific in my accomplishments. (Not that I don't already consider you my muse—because I do—but I long to have you close by all the time.) Have you ever thought about what inspires you, Aubrey? I think about it a lot, and my thoughts always turn to you. You've made me view the world in a different light. No, more than that—you've helped me actually *see* light again where previously there had been darkness for month after endless month. I don't think you're aware of the profound effect you've had on my life.

Two months ago, I was prone to coming unhinged and flying apart without a moment's notice. You've grounded me in a way you'll never understand—renewed my confidence and restored the lightness in my heart. I wish I could explain, but I hardly understand it myself…wait, my email alert is chirping with an email from you! It's so late, I wasn't expecting to hear from you again before bed. I can't wait to read your words, so I'll close here.

Yours and yours alone,

~Daniel

xoxoxo…

Hello, my sweetheart. Saturday night, and I'm moping around the condo looking forward to Monday. What is my life? I've had a rather unfortunate epiphany which somehow I managed to avoid thinking about yesterday. We've had our final tutorial together. It pains me that I'll never get to see you in action like that again. Your eyes light up when you discuss literature. Yesterday was no exception. It was wonderful watching you come alive as you discussed *All's Well That Ends Well* with your peers.

(And did you get a load of Cara? Wasn't that shocking? I've seen that side of her from time to time in our meetings. I don't know why she feels the need to put on the bimbo routine…)

The gift you all chipped in on was very thoughtful, too. Now I know what secret you were keeping, and I forgive you for holding out on me. You were right not to tell me. The fact remains, though, that one of the things I enjoyed most this semester is over. Will we still have fascinating conversations about books and authors we love when classes come to an end? God, I hope so…

Saying that—when classes come to an end—is surreal now. I can't believe we're almost there. Monday, two days from now—it's the LAST CLASS! What will we do when we walk out of that room and you're launched into exam hell as we wait for April 30 and the final for Martin's class? We won't see each other at all, nor should we—you'll be busy studying, and I want you to focus on your exams—but the thought of all that time apart is awful. Ten days? Jesus. And I thought Easter weekend was never-ending!

On the other hand, one more class and we're free of the very thing that's kept us apart all these long weeks. Well, not entirely free, but it's the beginning of the end, which allows us to finally contemplate "the beginning" for us, and surely that's good enough.

I suppose I need to change my mindset. This is our final "test." The last obstacle we have to cross before what can only be called sweet victory. And I fully intend to do a victory dance. With you. Naked. Bed optional. (What did you say the night of our first kiss? You were afraid we'd end up in the back seat doing a naked mambo? That's exactly what my victory dance will be—a naked mambo. I will start selecting the music tonight.)

And speaking of music, I've just listened to your CD and read the notes you wrote. So incredibly beautiful. Can I tell you my favorite part? I'm sure you could easily guess, but I'll tell you anyway. The Ingrid Michaelson song and the words you wrote to accompany it—

"You can catch me, Daniel. I will let you—that's how much I love you. I hope you understand the significance of those words—how hard they are for me to say. For me, they are the weightiest of all…"

Do you have any idea how I felt when I read those lines, Aubrey? Knowing you'll allow yourself to be vulnerable enough to let me help you is the greatest gift you could give me. So now all I can think about is how to be there for you over the many days we'll be apart. How can I let you know I'm there rooting for you and cheering you on as you work through the final days of your university career? Surely there's a more meaningful way, other than emails and phone calls, to remind you each and every day how much I love and cherish you.

Without spending any money.

Damn you.

(I'm shaking my fist at you right now.)

But you know I'm creative and stubborn as fuck (sorry to say, you've met your match, poppet) and I've got the acorn of an idea rolling around in my head, which I fully intend to put into action tomorrow. I've cleared my busy schedule (HAHA!) and will spend the day preparing a wonderful surprise for you. If I'm to get it finished tomorrow, though, I'll have to make an early start of it, so I'm going to turn in now and set my alarm for the butt crack of dawn.

I hope you're having a good weekend. I miss you horribly.

Yours,

~Daniel

xoxoxo…

SUNDAY, APRIL 19

How's my beautiful girl this evening? I'm exhausted. I was right to assume this little idea of mine would take some time to execute, but I've done it. All my ducks are in a row.

Here's my plan: I'm going to make you a card for every day we'll be apart until the end of exams — one for you to open every day. I've been all over hell's half acre with my camera today, taking pictures of all the places we've been during our "courtship." Then, late this afternoon, I settled in to do some reading, looking for appropriate literary references to accompany the pictures. I'm hoping to give the cards to you tomorrow, before our ten-day separation begins.

Cool idea, right? My grandfather would be proud. (Actually, the more I think about it, the more I realize he'd probably tell me to stop faffing around and get some work done. But it's too late to back out now.) I hope you'll enjoy opening each card and find the memories inspired by the pictures and words just as wonderful as I do.

For now, I must close. Before I turn in, I still have to write the individual messages inside the cards, and I have another early start tomorrow — a morning meeting with my dad. I called him earlier to let him know I'm really busy and might not be able to make it, but he insisted that he had something important to discuss. Ever the man of mystery, he wouldn't tell me what it was about.

I suppose meeting with him now is a good idea, anyway. I'd like to get his okay to use the cottage for the May 1st weekend. Fingers crossed he's in a good mood and feeling conciliatory because I've got my heart set on taking you up there. I feel comfortable and at home at the cottage, and it's far enough away from Toronto and the chaos that's surrounded us for the last couple of months that I can't help thinking it's the perfect locale for our first weekend together.

It's also really beautiful. I can already imagine you lying naked in front of the fire as you hold your hand out, beckoning me to join you. This is not a fantasy I'm prepared to abandon. I can't wait to give you the greatest of all pleasures — to worship your body the way I worship your heart, your soul, and your intellect.

I'll see you in sixteen hours. Yes, I'm counting. No, I don't care if you think I'm a lunatic. Yes, I love you with every fiber of my being.

~Daniel

xoxoxo…

MONDAY, APRIL 20

My beautiful Aubrey,

I have to tell you—I'm so glad I'm not sharing these letters with you right now because then you would see how truly pathetic I am and you'd likely run screaming for the hills. My misery is unparalleled this evening. The next ten days are stretching out before me like a dark abyss. (Is that redundant? I think it is. Is there such a thing as a bright abyss? Probably not.) Clearly, as I imagine spending ten days without seeing you, I've become a gibbering idiot. Not attractive.

And so, how do I cope? I turn to the book of love letters to try to find someone with greater gibbering idiocy than my own, of course. All I can say is, thank God for John Keats and his epic love letters to Fanny Brawne. His affection for her turned him into a lovesick wretch. Case in point—

"I cannot exist without you—I am forgetful of everything but seeing you again—my life seems to stop there—I see no further. You have absorb'd me. I have a sensation at the present moment as though I were dissolving…I have been astonished that men could die martyrs for religion—I have shudder'd at it—I shudder no more—I could be martyr'd for my religion—love is my religion—I could die for that—I could die for you. My creed is love and you are its only tenet—you have ravish'd me away by a power I cannot resist."

See what I mean? Now I can play the "holier than thou" card. *Good God, man. Pull yourself together! She's just a woman. They're a dime a dozen!* And if you think that's truly how I feel as I contemplate not seeing you for a full week and a half, then I've done an abysmal job of communicating my feelings for you.

Truth be told, I think I've over-communicated, at least on paper, and certainly in these letters—but the caveat, of course, is the fact that you're not seeing these letters. Even so, I'm certain I must have exhausted every possible word on the subject of my feelings while writing those cards last night. They started poetically enough, but by the last couple, I'm sure simply saying "See yesterday's card" or "Ditto" would have sufficed. Broken record? Absolutely. Do I care? Fuck no.

I hope you like them, Aubrey. The look on your face today when I gave them to you and explained what they were was a wonderful reward in itself (once you'd realized I hadn't spent a single cent making them, of course). You can't blame me for being annoyed by this damn no-gifts rule. Call me Huffy McHufferson as much as you like—once this stupid countdown is over, I'm going to blow the bank on you. But for now, I'm determined not to go back on my word.

Hopefully, having a daily card to open will sustain you during these days apart. I worry about you. It's such an important time. It would be so easy to lose focus now, so close to the end, and I know how important maintaining your Honors standing is. Now, to cap everything off, there's this business with the Graduate Student office calling you in for an interview. I don't pretend to know what's going on. Fingers crossed this isn't anything serious. I'm doing my best not to worry. I hope you're managing to stay calm, too. We're so close to the finish line.

Speaking of which, I got the okay from my dad to go to the cottage next weekend. I've decided to keep our destination a surprise. I have a couple of other ideas up my sleeve to surprise you with as well. (One of which definitely has a little to do with blowing the bank—so I'm DEFINITELY not telling you about that one.)

So now that my dad's given me (us) the stamp of approval to use the cottage, I can begin fantasizing about our time together up there in earnest, knowing that whatever scenario I cook up could very well become a reality, and not just a figment of my inflamed imagination. I'm over the moon at the prospect.

Well, I think I'll close there and get a head start on the aforementioned fantasies. Looking forward to hearing from you tomorrow after you open your first card, which, if I remember correctly, has a picture of Martin's classroom on the front. That classroom is simultaneously beloved and hateful to me: it was there that I saw you for the first time, but it's also one of the places I've been forced to conceal my love for you, a love which I'm eager to shout from the rooftops.

I hope you sleep well, my angel.

Talk to you tomorrow,

~Daniel Huffy McHufferson

xoxoxo…

Hi there, my lovely,

It's coming up to midnight. I just spoke to you on the phone. Hearing the plaintive tone in your voice was heartbreaking, and it's a wonder I'm not in my car right now driving up there to get you. You don't realize how difficult it is for me to be the strong one, sticking to my guns and placating you, when all I want to do is crumble, telling myself one night together won't hurt anyone.

I won't crumble. Not now. We've come so far and victory is so close. I'm allowing myself this moment, at 11:52 on a Wednesday night, to feel relief. I think it's the first time in a couple of months that my shoulders aren't stuck somewhere around my ears. I can feel the tension draining from my body. Things went well during your interview with Aaron O'Connor; Cara doesn't pose a threat; I had a successful meeting with my adviser, who seems to think I'm getting back on track with my paper; and soon we'll be home free.

In two-hundred hours, give or take a few (yes, I really am counting the hours until we can be together next Friday), we will drive far away from here and finally be a couple, in every sense, including the most mundane ones. Watching TV, going for walks, preparing meals — even the most routine activities won't be dull with you by my side.

Of course, I have some special treats planned, as well. As you know, I've been to Orillia today. What you don't know is why I was there. You see, I bought a boat. It'll be our own floating sanctuary, one we can bring back to Toronto with us and dock at the island for those times when we need an escape from the madness of the city. Doesn't that sound wonderful? I plan to take you for a spin around the lake next weekend. I'm sure after one sunset outing, you'll be won over.

Do I think I'll need to win you over? Yes. I know you. You'll freak out when you see the boat, for a multitude of reasons, not the least of which is the cost, but you'll be pleased to know, I exercised a measure of restraint. It's not brand new, and therefore wasn't exorbitantly priced. Because it's not new, it needs some work, so I've left the boat up in Orillia to be refurbished and detailed. I'm naming her after you, of course. *Poppet.*

Taking this sunset cruise is, of course, predicated on the fact that we'll actually be able to drag ourselves out of bed. What do you think, Aubrey? Once we're together, naked and warm, our bodies pressed together under the sheets, making love, holding each other as we sleep, and awakening to make love again—will there be time and inclination for something as mundane as a sunset cruise of the lake? Oddly enough, I sincerely hope so. Hell, there's nothing stopping us from christening the boat while we're out there…

Right, it's gone midnight and my eyes are burning. That was an awfully long drive today. I'll close here, with visions of you on the boat at sunset, the evening breeze tickling your hair as you gaze at me lovingly. Wait…you're unbuttoning your shirt…here, let me help you with that…

Your loving sailor,

~Daniel

xoxoxo…

SUNDAY, APRIL 26

My darling girl,

I open tonight with a few words from Gustave Flaubert (who, I've decided, may be my emotional doppelgänger):

"I am entirely UNDONE since your departure; it seems to me as if I had not seen you for ten years… We separated at the moment when many things were on the point of coming to our lips. All the doors between us two are not yet open."

When I stumbled across this letter, it struck a chord with me. The line about all the doors not being open yet makes me think of our dual isolation and the circumstances which have kept us apart, and yet not *driven* us apart. For almost a week now, we've shared only phone calls, texts and emails, and the coming days promise more of the same. We're not giving up, though, and I, for one, feel more determined than ever to dedicate myself entirely to loving you deeply and faithfully and *sharing everything*, a notion which leads quite nicely into my next point…

I spoke to Penny this evening. She's back, and full of excitement about the plans and arrangements she was able to take care of for the wedding, but obviously extremely happy to be back with Brad. She mentioned something during our chat — well, dug for information, I suppose is a better way of putting it — about whether I might consider bringing you to England for the wedding. I told her you'll already be over there visiting family, and that I hadn't broached the topic of you joining me, for a couple of reasons. First of all, I didn't want to be presumptuous — Penny hadn't invited you — but furthermore, you'll be with your family, and I'd hate to interfere with your holiday plans and impose my family's events on you. I'm leery of putting you on the spot.

Having said that, I'd love nothing more than to have you on my arm at Penny and Brad's wedding. It's sure to be an amazing day, and one I'd dearly love to share with you. Anyway, Penny's decided she's quite happy to put you on the spot (no surprise there), so she's going to contact you at some point to invite you, and I'll wait on tenterhooks for her to get her shit together, hoping that in the meantime your relatives in the UK don't create an airtight itinerary with no escape clauses.

Well, my beauty, five more sleeps and we will be together. We can do this. In the week ahead, you'll be preoccupied with finishing your exams, and I've been roped into helping Penny and Brad finish painting their main floor and spare room. Counting days will give way to counting hours, and before you know it, our reunion will be upon us. We will look back on this separation and laugh. One day we will say, "Remember when…"

One day, my love. One day soon.

Until then, I remain faithfully, yours. My heart and I are keeping your precious love, which consoles me daily, safely tucked away.

~Daniel

xoxoxo…

My gorgeous, sexy girl,

How ridiculous, forcing my fingers to tap out this mundane message after the journey they took today. What a divine expedition—from your lovely face to your neck, then lower, across the gloriously creamy expanse of skin lying in wait behind those five tiny buttons, and beyond…

It was so amazingly unexpected, spending those few stolen hours together. I can't seem to stop sifting through the details, reliving the tiniest moments, all precursors to our weekend away and what, I now know (as if I didn't before), will culminate in perfect bliss.

Do you want to know what I love, Aubrey? I'll tell you. In no particular order—neither chronological nor "most to least" (nor vice versa, for that matter. Don't look for logic, for there is none.)—these are the things I love:

Your lips.

Your hands.

Polka dots—yellow polka dots, in particular I adore.

Your breasts. God, don't get me started…

Your touch.

Your kisses. There are never enough. Ten is not enough. A hundred wouldn't be enough…a thousand…never enough. Etc.

Your incredible ass.

Did I mention your breasts? Ah yes, I see I did. Moving on.

The tiny silk bow at the top of your panties.

Your tongue.

YOUR YOGA PANTS.

The way your eyelashes fluttered this afternoon in the heat of the moment…in the heat of those few wonderful moments.

Your hair, tumbling across my chest as you slept. (I'm looking at a picture of this on my phone as I type. You don't know I took this picture, but you'll find out on Friday.)

Your lovely nipples, which I realize brings the topic around to your breasts again, but I hate to speak in vague generalities. Allow me to elucidate: you have the most perfectly delicious, pink nipples…

The arch of your back as I kissed your breasts for the first time, and the way you slipped your fingers through my hair, tugging hard.

Your lips forming my name as I touched you.

Your eyes.

The way your breath tickled my neck as you gasped with pleasure.

Your nails! I'll never tire of the feel of your nails on my back. Exquisite.

Your arms. Your legs. Your feet. Your toes. Your cheeks. Your ears. Your perky nose… (That rhyme was entirely unintended, by the way, albeit terribly "adorable," as you're fond of calling me…)

All of this. All of this and more, I love.

You.

I love you, my beautiful Aubrey.

(I'm also a huge fan of Penny. I'm sure you're with me on that. She gave us a precious gift today, wouldn't you say?)

As for her finally giving you the wedding invitation, I hope you're as thrilled as I am at the prospect of being together when she and Brad marry. Frankly, I feel as if I could explode with anticipation. There's so much ahead of us…so many things to do and see and experience together.

You know, after today, I feel more greedy than ever — wanting to be with you, wanting to keep you all to myself, knowing I can't possibly do that and desperately wanting to at the same time. There are so many more things that I have to learn about you, so many more undiscovered aspects of you to love. We've been in our "ready position" for so long, just waiting for that starter's pistol. Knowing our journey toward mutual discovery is really in its infancy excites me beyond words.

I've decided Julie was right in March, when she said we were lucky to have the time to get to know each other before embarking on an intimate relationship. I see now how much more meaningful our time together will be this weekend, knowing how deeply I care for you. God, that sounds so trite. I am literally beyond words, at this point, to communicate to you how much I love you. I need another medium. What do you think? Dance? No, a dance would render me ridiculous, even to myself. I'll leave the dancing business to Julie, shall I? How about a song? Now that's actually an interesting idea…one I think I'll ponder. In fact, I think I'll give that some serious thought right away. After I phone you, of course. :)

~Daniel (AKA, the man who loves you from your head to your toes and adores all the delicious stops in between.)

xoxoxo…

WEDNESDAY, APRIL 29

Hello, sweetheart,

You know, I've come to the conclusion that this weekend will be amazing, but there is one tiny caveat. It can only be amazing if the effort of pulling everything together doesn't kill me first. It's a good thing I have so many people in my corner helping me out. Today, I've talked on the phone with Patty, my dad, Brad, Penny (twice), Jeremy, Julie, and even Matt, every single phone call revolving around the next four days. It's absurd.

I called Patty just to let her know we'd be using the cottage this weekend—not that I needed her permission, but I felt compelled to let her know. She's excited for us and wishes us well, of course. I'll never be able to explain to her how much I appreciate and value her support. She's so looking forward to getting to know you better. (I hope the feeling is mutual.)

My talk with my dad didn't actually have to do with the weekend (with the exception of him reminding me about a few details when it comes to opening and closing the cottage—ever the pragmatist, my father). The reason I called him was to find out if he'd issued you an invitation to his party on Friday night. It turns out he still hasn't done that. At least he got his shit together and had your invitation printed, but with the way he's dragging his heels, I'm afraid you'll have made other plans by the time he invites you. I want to knock his block off sometimes.

Aside from my call to him, every other phone conversation had to do with the logistics of the next few days. Brad's lending me his truck so I can pick up the boat tomorrow and bring it to the cottage. Penny's coming with me to keep me company during the journey.

She's also bringing lasagna to store in the fridge at the cottage, so you and I will have a meal ready to eat on the weekend. I've also secured her promise to help me "spruce up the place" in preparation for our arrival on Saturday.

As for Jeremy, I've decided to follow my grandfather's footsteps and make sure you have some flowers waiting at home for you when you finish your exam tomorrow, but I'm bound by this damn promise I made, so I can't buy you flowers. The only alternative is to pick wild ones. Penny is putting a bouquet of spring flowers together from her garden and Jeremy has agreed to deliver them, along with one final card, to your residence for me while Penny and I are up north. Of course, this arrangement necessitated a call to Matt to make sure he'll be around when Jeremy drops by.

Finally, there's Miss Harper. I've been thinking about what I wrote in last night's letter. Though I was speaking in jest, I thought it might be kind of cool to write you a song, but given everything else I have going on over the next couple of days, I don't have the time. Between the trek up north tomorrow and then marking through the evening and getting through all the chaos of Friday—and somehow working in a trip to La Vie en Rose and to Swarovski to pick up a couple of surprises—there aren't enough hours in the day.

Instead of starting from scratch and writing you a song, I'm cheating a little. I decided to find one of your favorite poems and put that to music instead. I called Julie to pick her brain, and she told me about your fondness for Pablo Neruda. Needless to say, I did a little research, and I've found one of his poems that would perfectly suit a sunset cruise on Sunday. It's called "In My Sky at Twilight," and I've already worked out the melody.

I hope you'll like it. Despite the melancholy tone, the words are very compelling. I'm particularly taken by the third stanza. I can't wait to sing those words to you, though to be honest, I may have to shout that stanza. I think it's become my new mantra. It goes something like this.

You.

Are.

Mine.

MINE.

Hope you're okay with that. I sound awfully possessive, don't I? Does it help to hear me say in return, that I am one-hundred percent, unequivocally yours, my love?

I hope so.

Yours.

YOURS,

~Daniel

xoxoxo…

P.S. I won't be writing tomorrow. I know I won't have time during the day, and I need to focus on your exam tomorrow night without distractions. I'll be back on Friday, though, at which point we'll be counting down the minutes. I can't wait.

Hi, my lovely girl,

I have NEVER been so happy to turn the page of a calendar as I was this morning. May. It's FINALLY May!

I mustn't stay up too late writing. We have a long drive ahead of us tomorrow, after all, and I'm going to need plenty of energy for the events I have planned. But I have to spill a little ink, first to apologize for the way things played out this evening. I had no idea Sabrina would be dropping off her parents at my dad's reception, and I'm truly sorry her arrival caught you off guard. More than that, though, I'm sorry I didn't tell you she was back in town. If I'd mentioned that, perhaps you would have been less taken aback when you saw her walk through the door tonight, and your evening wouldn't have been ruined.

I'm not purposely treating you like a fragile vase that might break with the slightest jostle, Aubrey, I hope you know that. You can hold your own with Sabrina, and with anyone for that matter (Jesus, don't I know it…). No, what I fear is the destruction of the tenuous connection between us and the potentially damaging effects of the stupid things that keep happening to us. After our talk tonight, though, I realize I have to stop trying to build a cocoon around us. We can't avoid conflict, and my constant desire to circumvent issues only makes things worse in the long run.

We will face challenges and we will have arguments and squabbles. After all we've endured, I have to learn to trust in the strength of our love. It's not a case of thinking you don't love me. It's just that there's something intangible about our love. I think sometimes I need to feel its solidity—its concreteness—in order to truly trust it. I hate admitting that, but I know it's simply a result of the situation we've found ourselves in. With time, I know this feeling will pass. I'm sure living out our relationship in the real world instead of in my imagination or in the pages and pages of these letters will help.

Please forgive me for being an ass. I will make it up to you. This weekend I will focus on setting things right and proving my worthiness in every possible way. In fact, I'm so intent on the deeds that must follow all these many, many words I've written leading up to this weekend that I've completely run out of things to say.

When I see you tomorrow, Aubrey, this will be my most ardent desire…to give you a thousand kisses everywhere…Until then, I send you a thousand imaginary kisses…everywhere…

Yours, in word, and soon, in deed,

~Daniel

xoxoxo…

My beautiful Aubrey,

Well, here I am. The morning after the most wonderful weekend of my life. It's six a.m. I know. I'm crazy. I only got about four hours of sleep. That nap we took yesterday afternoon must have messed up my internal clock. Not that I'm complaining. It was the best nap ever. Falling asleep completely naked with you in my arms at two in the afternoon is certainly not something you'll find me regretting.

In fact, I don't regret a single second of this weekend. I wouldn't change a solitary detail. Not one. Even Saturday night — making love to you for the first time in front of the fire — maybe I should kick myself for the way things played out. My anxiousness could have entirely ruined our evening, but how can I entertain a single regretful feeling about the way you comforted me? I've never been more grateful for another person's presence of mind so entirely in my life. What a beautiful, caring soul you are. You are also incredibly sexy. You quickly obliterated any remaining anxiety I might have felt the second you straddled me.

Hello? Anxiety, shmanxiety!

You don't understand how sexy you are, which I'm sure makes you even sexier. Knowing what I do now, I can't help thinking back over the semester. It's a very good thing I've been lost entirely in the world of my imagination. If I had the very real (and hot as fucking hell) image of you standing before the fire slowly undressing lodged in my mind's eye all semester, we wouldn't have made it through that first tutorial. I would have dismissed everyone but you within five minutes and insisted on tutoring you within an inch of your life.

With my tongue.

And other things.

Other very hard things.

One of these things is actually getting hard right now as I think about how it felt to touch you for the first time. Slipping my fingers between your creamy soft thighs that first time — that moment is emblazoned in my memory, and will be forever, I'm sure. It's second only to the feeling of looking into your eyes as I finally, FINALLY experienced the unparalleled ecstasy of moving inside you.

"Transcendent" is a word that's bandied around at times like this, as a lover tries to properly articulate the emotional heft of such a moment. Well, it's safe to say that even the word "transcendent" is a feeble description of how it felt to connect with you like that, Aubrey. And making love to you in the middle of the night — the quiet passion of that experience — it almost brought tears to my eyes. Maybe a "real" man shouldn't admit things like that, but I'm inclined to argue that only a real man would allow himself to acknowledge such depth of feeling and have the courage to share it with the woman he loves.

(At least that's my story, and I'm damn well sticking to it.)

For me the past two days were full of moments like these. I've never enjoyed my time at the cottage so much. I'm sure the memories of our weekend will color every experience I have at the cottage from now on. How will I ever play pool there again? I'll try to line up a shot, and all I'll see is you lying there naked, rolling that damn eight ball in your hand and gazing up at me with those I-just-came-so-hard eyes. Good God. Balls will fly everywhere.

Interpret as you will.

And how can I possibly see that bed (where I shortened your life measurably — sorry about that) as a mere place to sleep, or look at that shower stall the same way again?

Actually, I'm quite happy to never look at that shower — or any shower for that matter — the same way again. Showering alone was becoming a decidedly unfortunate activity. Henceforth, I must never shower alone. This will take some rejigging of schedules etc., but I must always have you with me when I shower from this point forward.

Deal? Deal.

I could blither on ad nauseam about how hot you are, and about how great it is having frequent and mind-blowing sex with you, and how happy I am knowing I won't have to eat another tomato ever again. I could rave on and on about your amazing lips and talented tongue, your soft breasts and exquisite ass, but that's not all this weekend meant to me.

(Cue: your stunned face—I know it's positively shocking…)

The past two days were an absolute affirmation of what I've been telling you for weeks, or at least what I've been thinking…I'm starting to lose track of what I've pondered here, and what I've actually told you. This is not good. Anyway, what I mean to say is you've brought such light and laughter into my life. For so long I've wished I could spend my days reveling in the fun of your company. As I told you yesterday, I think of the day I heard you and Matt laughing behind your apartment door at Jackman, and how desperately I wished that were me instead of him. And now it is.

I'm no longer on the other side of that door. In fact, all of the doors are open between us. These last couple of days were exactly what I'd been wishing for. Going for walks, playing in the games room, cooking and eating together, watching movies, boating…even being forced to chase you around the cottage nude because you stole my clothes—every moment was pure, unadulterated fun.

I'm not naïve enough to believe that we won't continue to have trials and tribulations—every couple does—but you deal with everything so pragmatically. (At least it seems so to me. Perhaps you'd disagree.) I know there will be bumps in the road, but I'm sure we can face anything together.

I've searched in vain through the letters in this book of my grandfather's, desperate for some passage that will help me to articulate how amazed I am that we stand here with a future before us. It's been a frustrating journey to get to the point we've reached. It's a journey that's tested us, taking what started as attraction and a mutual interest and allowing it to become what I want to call complete communion. I can no longer imagine my life without you in it. That's why I gave you the key to the condo, Aubrey, and why I hope you'll use it.

What I'd dearly love is for you to move in lock, stock, and barrel, but I won't pressure you. Doing that would get me nowhere fast, and in fact would most likely be counterproductive; but it's difficult for me to keep my peace when I see no good reason for us to remain apart. It's entirely safe for me to purge my deepest wish on this page, though. My deepest wish is this: I want you here. Every day. Always. Full-time.

I know I'll talk to you soon and hopefully see you, as well. If all goes well, I'll be able to convince you to come back here today so we can start christening the condo. Plus, I really need to shower, and how can I do that if you're not here? A deal is a deal.

All my love,

~Daniel

xoxoxo…

Update: Monday, May 4, 11:30 p.m.

My lovely girl,

I must be crazy because I've left you alone in bed to sneak off to the office and write. You're asleep, though, so it's not like I've actually abandoned you. You're dead to the world—even snoring a little. It's very cute. I don't blame you for conking out. I think it might have been the four glasses of wine and the…"after dinner activities."

You're absolutely exhausted.

Anyway, the reason I've come in here to write is that I was lying in bed thinking about this afternoon. Telling you a little more about my anxiety issues today—explaining all of my foibles and the events in my past which precipitated me developing these various eccentricities—was so incredibly liberating. It was also very eye-opening. You said you can see why I would have kept all of this to myself, but that it's important for you to understand these things about me. *Of course* it's important.

You bought yourself a notebook today so you can begin to write for enjoyment. You said it was only fair—I write about you, so shouldn't you be able to write about me? I made you promise to continue telling me everything as well, and not just turning to the pages of your notebook when you felt the need to vent. What a hypocrite I am.

As much as I hate to admit it, I suppose writing all of my feelings here might be impeding me from sharing things with you as fully as I should. And so, although it pains me, I've decided it's time to give my keyboard a rest. As my grandfather used to tell me when I was a kid, no one can read my mind. I have a tongue in my head and it's my responsibility to use it.

Instead of pouring my heart out here, I'll pour it out to you, my poppet, just as I did today. I think this will be good for my mental health. Beyond that, I believe it'll be beneficial for our relationship. With that decision made, all that's left is to share these letters with you, and I will — but not yet. Sharing them will be a gift, but more than that, it will be a daring leap of faith. I will know when the time is right. I look forward to that day, whenever it may be.

It's difficult to know how to close three months' worth of thoughts and feelings. Maybe simplicity is best. Please know that I cherish you with my whole heart. I don't know how long these letters will remain under wraps, but until the day I share them with you, I will make sure you know — both with my words and my actions — that I love you.

Happily, I can now close my laptop, safe in the knowledge that in less than two minutes, I'll crawl back into bed and pull you into my arms. You'll then proceed to drool contentedly on my chest for the next seven hours.

And all will be right with the world.

Yours, in every conceivable way,

~Daniel

xoxoxo…

Part Four

The Record of My Heart

SUNDAY, NOVEMBER 1ST

Hey, gorgeous,

As you can see, it's been a while since I checked in here. We've been together for almost nine months. During that time, we've been through a storm, Aubrey—a storm, a tempest, a fucking Chinook—call it what you will. I would argue that our relationship hasn't just survived this storm, it's triumphed in the face of it. Our love for each other has endured many trials, several of which threatened to chase me back here to the comfort of these blank pages. I resisted this compulsion every time.

That day we had the awful fight about Eli, for example, it would have been so easy to rage at a blank page, filling it with complaints and misery. I stopped myself. Instead, I went for a long walk and then listened to some music, keeping those thoughts locked in my head so that when they eventually did spill, they would be words shared with you rather than with a computer file. I'm so glad I made that decision.

I wish I'd used a similar approach to deal with my summertime crisis involving Nicola. I truly believed you weren't remotely interested in hearing her name, which is why I resisted telling you what I'd found out about her. But choosing not to share with you and opting not to purge my feelings on paper had a disastrous effect. The bad dreams and constant anxiety were inevitable.

Having you by my side when I confronted Nicola and finally put the past to rest was an unparalleled experience. I felt so safe knowing you were there supporting me. More importantly, it reminded me of the importance of communicating with you openly. I'm convinced that our ability to tell each other anything—to share everything without fear of judgment—is what brings us to where we are today.

And where is that, you ask? Let me tell you.

You've gone off to the theater to watch and review *The Boys in the Photograph*, and I'm alone, nursing a glass of wine and rereading this collection of journals and letters, and pondering one of the most intricately planned proposals imaginable. I say that as if it's a nuisance figuring out how best to propose to you, but I don't mean that at all. What I mean is, I want it to be perfect. I've always been a romantic fool, but the pressure to make a proposal not just meaningful, but *unforgettable* is overwhelming. But trust me when I say I've done my homework to make sure I don't screw up.

I've got the ring—carefully designed with suggestions from your mother and Julie and some invaluable input from Patty (you'll understand that when you see the ring for yourself). I've chosen the date on which I'll propose (a Friday the thirteenth, no less), and I have a plan in place to get together with your father in Calgary when I head out west to attend the Renaissance symposium next week. I'm determined to meet him and secure his blessing before asking for your hand. The only thing left to do is to craft the words to the proposal, which I'm sure will cause me a fair amount of angst because, regardless of what I say, I'll never be able to properly communicate the multitude of reasons behind my desire to spend the rest of my life with you—at least not succinctly…

However, when I ask you to marry me, I'll be gazing into your eyes, and when you look at me, you will see my soul, as you have since the day our eyes first met. Even without words, I have no doubt my feelings for you are always written on my face, in every doting smile, every fiery gaze, every loving glance. Having said that, I often wonder if you truly understand the depth of my love for you—how much you've changed my life.

That's where this book comes in. For months, I waffled about letting you read the journals and letters I wrote in the spring. So many times I could have given them to you. I almost gave you the entire collection when you went to England. I was so desperate for you to have a piece of me with you, but every time I imagined you reading them, my mind would wander back to that day when Patty showed me my grandfather's letters, the pages yellowed with age and smudged from years of reading and rereading. How could I possibly give you a collection of love letters as a PDF file? To do that seemed entirely dispassionate.

In the end, I held off, revealing only those early journal entries. The summer went by with the question constantly plaguing me: Is now the right time? How about now?

I finally made the decision after our return from England. That trip convinced me once and for all that you are the one I'm meant to be with. Forever. On Labor Day weekend when we went boating, and I hinted at our future together, your wonderful reaction led me to believe that you'd accept a proposal. At first, I thought that might be an appropriate time to share the letters with you, but I was reluctant to put pressure on you by giving them to you at that point. And so I decided to wait, giving them to you after I've proposed, and you've (hopefully) accepted.

While rereading every single word I wrote during those long weeks in the spring, I've cringed, laughed, shaken my head and wondered if I'm crazy to let you read them, but at this point, what do I have to hide? You know me, Aubrey, better than anyone else in the world — better than I know myself sometimes.

So here I sit, holding a pile of typed pages, but tomorrow I'll take these pages in to be bound into a book, my gift to you — *The Record of My Heart*.

You may wonder how I landed on this title. It actually came to me as I mulled over what passage to use as an epigraph. I wanted to choose something meaningful to inscribe on the opening page, some words to express not just the purpose of this book, but also the very essence of the many, many words within. I pored over the book of love letters my grandmother gave me and scanned volume after volume of poetry. And then, this afternoon, once you'd left for the theater, I was sitting in the bedroom and I saw that book on the shelf — the one you bought me back in May — Tagore's *The Gardener*. I flipped through it, and within a few minutes, the perfect passage revealed itself, a selection of lines from Verse 16:

"Hands cling to hands and eyes linger on eyes: thus begins the record of our hearts…

…It is a game of giving and withholding, revealing and screening again; some smiles and some little shyness, and some sweet useless struggles…

…No mystery beyond the present; no striving for the impossible; no shadow Behind the charm; no groping in the depth of the dark…

…It is enough what we give and get…

…This love between you and me is simple as a song."

This passage is perfect — most appropriate, given that this book chronicles the stirrings of my heart from the moment I set eyes on you. In all honesty, the entire verse captures the way I feel about you and about our love. We've had our fair share of struggles, but we always return to each other. That's all there is, Aubrey. You and me — the joy you bring to my life, a joy which I hope I'm able to return tenfold.

That's all there needs to be.

On the way home from Brad and Penny's last night, I told you how completely blessed and whole I feel having your love, light, and laughter in my life, and you blamed my sappiness on the drinks I'd consumed. Believe me, Aubrey, I would proclaim the same words without an ounce of alcohol in my blood, as in fact, I do, here and now. Whether sober, tipsy, or drunk as a skunk, I'm yours, for as long as you'll have me. I hope that's a very, very long time.

You've mentioned a couple of times that you hope you're as feisty as Patty when you're eighty. I hope you are, too. And I pray I'm beside you, holding your hand, seeing your eighty-year-old feistiness with my own eyes — eyes which will look at you adoringly for as long as I live. If you say you'll be mine forever, I will try my utmost to make this a reality.

I will close there, for what else is there to say? I love you, and I look forward to asking for your hand in twelve days.

Adoringly yours,

Daniel

xoxoxo…

Thursday, November 12

Hi, sweetheart,

I'm in my hotel room, pen in hand, awake far too early again. In an hour or so, I'll be in a taxi, heading for the airport. Finally! I can't wait to get home. I've learned a lot and had a great time out here. BC is beautiful and the symposium was incredibly energizing, but you've never been far from my thoughts.

I'm glad I left a couple of blank pages at the end of this book. There's something else I feel compelled to add which I know will make you smile — a postscript of a sort, I suppose. A few weeks ago, you said you've missed me channeling Dr. Seuss, so imagine me in my hotel room last night, writing this poem — something else to add to the short anthology of horrid verse documenting the times we've been apart. (More and more, I realize it's best if you never leave my side.) Without further ado...

An Ode to Aubrey Price on the Eve of Friday the Thirteenth

I miss your eyes and eyelash flutter
I crave your mess; I miss your clutter
I miss your lips and breathy kisses
A drool-soaked shirt, my chest most misses.
I miss your hands, our fingers twined
(Your nails are also on my mind...)
I miss your legs; I miss your arms
I miss your soft, sweet nether-charms.
I miss your voice, your crazy jokes
Your puckered brows and sharp rib pokes.
I miss your cheeks, your ears, your nose
I even miss your frigid toes!

I miss your presence in a room
 Your antics always lift the gloom.
I miss you, but I feel you near
'Cause Thursday, well, it's almost here
And Friday night we'll celebrate
Nine months together— (I can't wait).
November's chill will fill the air
I'll keep you close and we won't care.
We'll hug and kiss, we'll dance and dine
And all I've missed will then be mine.
So when you wake on Friday morning
Please remember this small warning:
On Friday night, there'll be no slumber
'Cause thirteen is my lucky number.

Wretched, right? But it had to be done. Okay. It's time.
Close the book, my lovely. Close the book, and we'll start a new
one together. I look forward to filling endless blank pages with
you.

Yours, with infinite love and an insufferably romantic
affection,

Daniel

xoxoxo…

P.S. I've lost track of how many times I've written "xoxoxo…"
over the months in notes, emails, text messages, and now here, in
these letters. I've never meant that "dot, dot, dot" more than I
do at this very moment

I love you.

ACKNOWLEDGMENTS

A heartfelt thanks to the Omnific family, my #streetteam, my fabulous friends and wonderful family. Most importantly, to my readers, without whom this journey would not have been nearly as fun. Thank you.

~GG

ABOUT THE AUTHOR

Georgina Guthrie is a self-professed book hugger and compulsive diarist. Though GG now resides in Canada, she was born across the pond and still considers herself a Brit through and through, which may explain her frequent visits to her favorite local British import shop.

GG is often happiest when reading and writing, but she's just as likely to be found hanging out with friends and family, almost certainly with a glass of red wine in one hand a bag of cheese and onion crisps in the other.

Join Georgina on Twitter @georgey_girl

‹——⊶⊷——›New Adult Romance‹——⊶⊷——›

Three Daves by Nicki Elson
Streamline by Jennifer Lane
The Shades series: *Shades of Atlantis* & *Shades of Avalon* by Carol Oates
The Heart series: *Beside Your Heart, Disclosure of the Heart* & *Forever Your Heart*
by Mary Whitney
Romancing the Bookworm by Kate Evangelista
Flirting with Chaos by Kenya Wright
The Vice, Virtue & Video series: *Revealed, Captured, Desired* & *Devoted*
by Bianca Giovanni
Granton University series: *Loving Lies* by Linda Kage
Missing Pieces by Meredith Tate

‹——⊶⊷——›Paranormal & Fantasy Romance‹——⊶⊷——›

The Light series: *Seers of Light, Whisper of Light* & *Circle of Light* by Jennifer DeLucy
The Hanaford Park series: *Eve of Samhain* & *Pleasures Untold* by Lisa Sanchez
Immortal Awakening by KC Randall
The Seraphim series: *Crushed Seraphim* & *Bittersweet Seraphim* by Debra Anastasia
The Guardian's Wild Child by Feather Stone
Grave Refrain by Sarah M. Glover
The Divinity series: *Divinity* & *Entity* by Patricia Leever
The Blood Vine series: *Blood Vine, Blood Entangled* & *Blood Reunited*
by Amber Belldene
Divine Temptation by Nicki Elson
The Dead Rapture series: *Love in the Time of the Dead, Love at the End of Days* &
Love Starts with Z by Tera Shanley
The Hidden Races series: *Incandescent* (book 1) by M.V. Freeman
Something Wicked by Carol Oates
Chronicles of Midvalen: *Command the Tides* (book 1) by Wren Handman

‹——⊶⊷——›Romantic Suspense‹——⊶⊷——›

Whirlwind by Robin DeJarnett
The CONduct series: *With Good Behavior, Bad Behavior* & *On Best Behavior*
by Jennifer Lane
Indivisible by Jessica McQuinn
Between the Lies by Alison Oburia
Blind Man's Bargain by Tracy Winegar

‹——⊶⊷——›Erotic Romance‹——⊶⊷——›

The Keyhole series: *Becoming sage* (book 1) by Kasi Alexander
The Keyhole series: *Saving sunni* (book 2) by Kasi & Reggie Alexander
The Winemaker's Dinner: *Appetizers* & *Entrée* by Dr. Ivan Rusilko & Everly Drummond
The Winemaker's Dinner: *Dessert* by Dr. Ivan Rusilko
Client N° 5 by Joy Fulcher
The Enclave series: *Closer and Closer* (book 1) by Jenna Barton

Shackled by Debra Anastasia
Swim Recruit by Jennifer Lane
Sway by Nicki Elson
Full Speed Ahead by Susan Kaye Quinn
The Second Sunrise by Hannah Downing
The Summer Prince by Carol Oates
Whatever it Takes by Sarah M. Glover
Clarity (A *Divinity* prequel single) by Patricia Leever
A Christmas Wish (A *Cocktails & Dreams* single) by Autumn Markus
Late Night with Andres by Debra Anastasia
Poughkeepsie (enhanced iPad app collector's edition) by Debra Anastasia
Poughkeepsie (audio book edition) by Debra Anastasia
Blood Eternal (A Blood Vine series single, epilogue to series) by Amber Belldene
Carnaval de Amor (*The Winemaker's Dinner*, Spanish edition)
by Dr. Ivan Rusilko & Everly Drummond

coming soon from
OMNIFIC PUBLISHING

The Hidden Races series: *Illumination* (book 2) by M.V. Freeman
The Counterfeit by Tracy Winegar
The Embrace series: *Entwined* (book 3) by Cherie Colyer
The Adventures of Clarissa Hardy by Chloe Gillis
Where All Good Dreams Are Real by Jane Susann McCarter
The Ground Rules by Roya Carmen
Trouble Me by Beck Anderson